THE LONG JOURNEY HOME

A NOVEL

DOLORES DURANDO

ISBN 979-8-9866994-2-4

Cover and book design: Barbara Holiday
Published by N8tive Run Press, a subsidiary of N8tive Run Enterprises, 5007 Laurel Avenue, Grants Pass, OR 97527

DEDICATION

For Bill'n'Cathy with my love
and appreciation.
You light up my life.

ACKNOWLEDGEMENT

Again and again, my deepest appreciation
for my loyal, patient, indispensable editor,
Barbara Holiday,
who endeavors to make me better
and forgives me my spelling.

CHAPTER 1

It had snowed the night before and my breath hung in the frosty air. My feet crunched and sunk ankle-deep in a hidden hole. When, if ever, will this damn sidewalk be finished? It was cold and I hurried.

I usually opened early to get the place cleaned up and warm before the regulars came in, but today, as I neared the bar, I could see a couple of men who apparently had an even earlier start.

Slouched against the storm door, a tall, thin man stood waiting, his collar turned up to cover the shaggy black hair that showed beneath the cap pulled over his ears. His shabby coat hung from his shoulders and rested at the top of his overshoes.

His companion trailed behind and looked just as bad.

I pushed him aside as I opened the door to the small, dark bar that had been my livelihood and occasional entertainment for the last few years.

The odor of spilled beer, the lingering smoke of hand-rolled

Bull Durhams, a jar of pickled pigs feet starting to go bad, and the spittoons I had neglected to empty reminded me I had left early last night in anticipation of Bessie's pot roast. A pot roast like no other. Bessie, my Bessie, my wife of fifty-three years. The men crowded behind me and I flipped on the lights.

"Hell, Fritz, you sleep in? Yer late!"

"You keeping time on me, Helmer? Find a seat."

The men in their heavy work clothes settled themselves at the bar. Helmer, the tall one, I knew well. He was called the town drunk.

"Let's have one, Fritz, we're 'bout froze."

They sat hunched together with dirty splayed fingers holding their shot glasses. The melting snow on their overshoes created muddy splotches on the floor. I was glad I hadn't cleaned up last night.

"Hey, Fritz, let's have another one over here if you ain't too busy. Hurry it up." Laughing through his whiskers, Helmer added, "If you please. Yeah, let's have one more and then we better git on the job or Uncle Sam might fire us. Damn, but it's cold! Whyn't hell couldn't this ditch been dug before the ground froze up? The radio said there's a blizzard blowin' down from Canady."

"Don't know what yer bitchin' about," his buddy answered. "Ain't nuthin more than just a hard freeze. Thirty below ain't nuthin and Uncle Sam is payin' us thirty-five bucks a month to dig that damn water main. Hell, I ain't complainin'—me 'n the old lady wuz about to starve. Thank God for the WPA."

"Ya damned fool! Wuzn't God—it wuz Roosevelt!"

The door shoved open and a short, muscular man hurried in wearing a black and red plaid mackinaw, a sheriff's badge pinned on his chest. Before I could lay my bar towel down, his knuckles rapped.

"What will it be, Sheriff?" I asked, irritated.

"I need something good to keep me company. None of that rotgut you water down for your regulars. Maybe some of your private stash? Seagram's 7 Crown? I'm on my way to St. Paul on business, you know. Probably be back in a couple of days. Hurry it up—we Frenchmen don't like waiting. Hey, I heard a Norwegian is just a Swede with his brains knocked out. Any truth to that, Norsky?"

The sound of silver on the bar, the rustle of a paper sack, then a "See you later" was accompanied by his taunting laugh as the door closed.

"That cocky little bastard! He got some of my special stash all right—that bottle is about one-third pure Norsky piss. I was careful with the seal—he'll never notice."

"You said it right, Fritz. He hides behind that piece of tin, thinks he's King Shit because he runs that little two-cell jail over in Fosston. He should stick to pig farmin'—that's his speed. I can tell you from experience that he's too damned handy with that night stick, specially after he's had a few shots of 'shine. Hey, see anything of the Torgerson boys? Heard they went fishin'."

"Not yet, but I expect they'll be along real soon. Probably drove all night and want a drink to thaw out." I picked up the broom, which neither one seemed to notice.

"Yeah," Helmer said. "Them Torgerson boys. Hell, they ain't been boys for a while. It otta be agin' the law to be so damned good lookin'—tall, all that yella hair. They take after their ma—she wuz a knockout and still is."

His buddy spoke up. "Yep, Olaf is king of the hill, fer sure. He's whipped every son of a bitch in the country, and Orren is the lover boy that comforts their wimmin."

I had to laugh—those were pretty accurate descriptions.

"You fellas better drink up and get to work. You're late now and I want to clean up."

"One more and we're outta here, okay?" Helmer pleaded. "I wish I wuz wearin' that good-lookin' red 'n black mackinaw, ya know. I'd look good in that." As an afterthought, he added, "Charbeneau can pin that badge on his ass— wouldn't that fancy him up? But I'd settle for the bottle if Fritz hadn't pissed in it. He ruint a perfectly good bottle of whiskey." Interrupting himself, he said, "Hey, I saw Charbeneau's new tires Sadidday night."

"Where'd you see 'em, Helmer, over at the dance hall?"

"Yeah."

His sidekick stuck a wad in his lower lip and asked, "Well, what happened up there? I had my old lady over to her sister's Sadidday night. She had another kid—that makes six and the oldest is only eight. Rudy otta git out and git a job. She wuz screamin' an carryin' on all night. Me'n him went in the kitchen and got drunker'n hell. She had the kid before noon so I jist took my old lady home and slept it off. Guess she heard sumpthin on the party line about Charbeneau beatin' up on some kids. What happened, Helmer? Did you see anything?"

I hung up the bar towel and leaned over to listen.

"Well, damned if I know for sure, I wuz drunk too—drinkin' mine out of a fruit jar. I know the hall wuz packed and so thick with smoke that I could hardly see old Knute up there on the platform, his spit can on top of the pianna like always. Lars with that chaw of snoose—his spit can between his knees—damned if I know how he can work that harmonica. Then the other guy jist spittin' on the floor. Nobody danced close to that end. Somebody yelled, 'Can'tcha play nuthin' but them old-time waltzes? How about a polka or a shottish?' All them old grandmas sittin' along the wall, kids bawlin', tired 'n sleepy. My ears wuz bustin'."

"C'mon, c'mon. Git to it. We ain't got all days," his sidekick nagged.

"You wanta hear this or not?" Helmer asked.

"Fritz has 'bout scrubbed all the paint off the other end of this bar. He's gittin' itchy, but what the hell, let him scratch. I wanta hear."

"Well, my belly wuz on fire—musta got aholt of some bad hooch. I know I wuz gonna lose it so I pushed my way through the door and set down at the top of the steps, bent over, and let it go. Leaned up aside the wall and almost dozed off. Somebody stumbled agin me and when I stood up I saw a tall girl holdin' a little boy's hand headin' fer the toilet. That lantern above the door don't give much light, but I recognized the Torgerson girl and her little brother—Buddy, they call him—when they walked down the path. She's 'bout fifteen, I think. Them lanterns at the 'his' and 'hers' ain't much either, but they went on down anyway."

Helmer stopped for breath, and I leaned closer as he continued.

"The bright lights of a car parked right in front of the steps came on and this guy got out and opened the back door. I thought that wuz kinda funny 'cause he walked down behind the kids. I figgered he musta been drunker'n me because he wuz on the wrong path.

"Well, he stopped beside the toilet, and when the kids came out, he grabbed at the girl. But she pulled out of her coat and ran screaming for her ma, the boy tryin' to keep up. Well, he stumbled and fell down and the guy had him—the boy bawlin' for his sister. She turned around and came back and that son of a bitch got her too. She wuz screamin' 'Ma, Ma,' and fightin' and kickin' them long skinny legs, but he had her arm twisted behind her and he dragged them both up the path to his car."

Helmer stubbed out what was left of his cigarette and dropped it on the floor.

"What the hell wuz you doin'? Watchin' the show?"

"I yelled, 'Hey, you! What the hell you doin' with them kids?' He looked up and I saw it wuz Charbeneau."

"You shoulda run down them steps and cold-cocked that bastard," his drinking buddy snarled.

"I ain't no hero," Helmer said, "but I wuz nervin' myself up to do that when them big doors bulged open and the crowd piled out. I wuz sure glad 'cause I figgered on some help. You know how the music stops for an hour break at midnight and everybody eats whatever lunch they brung— you know how that goes. So the light shines out the big doors and when they heard the girl screamin' and saw it wuz Charbeneau, the car lights started to come on and people circled 'round him."

I tapped him on the shoulder and asked, "Fellas, can I sit in on this story?"

"Hell, yes, Fritz, pull up a stool. Where wuz you Sadidday night?"

"Home with my wife staying out of trouble. Go on, I'm listening."

Helmer struck a match on his shabby pants and tried to light a stubbed-out, hand-rolled cigarette and cussed as it fell to pieces.

"Well, as I wuz sayin', the girl is fightin' so hard he needs both hands, so he lets go of the boy and kicks him. The kid went down and jist laid there with his hands over his face and blood runnin' through his fingers. He wuz reachin' for his sister when Charbeneau shoved him in the car."

The shock and outrage was evident on Helmer's face as he remembered.

"Fritz, I could sure use a drink."

"Hell, no. Go on with your story. I want to hear it while you're still sober."

"You go to hell, Fritz. We shoulda gone to Sorenson's."

He dug into his pocket and pulled out an empty pack of cigarette papers, cussed some more, and threw the paper on the floor.

"The crowd all swarmin' around like when you step on a anthill—pushin', shovin' back and forth, cussin' each other loud enough to wake the dead. Everybody fightin' to git in the front for a better look.

"Helga wuz fightin' to get to the kids and nobody would give her an inch. She's beggin' 'Don't! Don't! Don't for God's sake. Don't hurt my kids. Please, please!' 'Bout broke my heart.

"Charbeneau yelled, 'Somebody take care of that,' and somebody did. Took three men to put Helga on the ground. Finally, she wuz choked off.

"Then the girl got it all. He wuz poundin' her with his fists tryin' to force her in the back seat. Them mothers and fathers with kids of their own were yellin' 'Let her have it. She's still movin'. Damn Norskies! Barnburners!' "

Helmer closed his eyes.

"They wuz crazy, like a pack of wolves with a bloody sheep."

He sat quiet for a minute, and I could hear his sidekick's rough breathing.

"Then," he continued, "I got scart, scart sober. I heard the thud-thud-thud of his nightstick and the girl went down. He stuffed her in the back seat too, and the crowd cheered. Cheered! I kin still hear 'em. Then he drove off.

"I saw Helga struggle to her feet, stagger to her car and follow. I hid under them porch steps with Knute and Lars 'til the mob broke up. They wuz whoopin' and dancin' in their overshoes there in the front with no music till 'round three o'clock.

"We wuz 'bout froze under them steps. It all seemed like a turrible dream. I couldn't git my brain 'round it. Sometimes when I wake up at night wantin'—hell, needin'!—a drink real bad, I can still smell them stinky lanterns, the sweat, the smoke, even the blood, and hear them kids screamin' and Helga beggin'."

His voice choked and he blew his nose on a bar towel, wiping the remnants on his sleeve.

"I wonder if she got the kids."

"Yeah, she got 'em," Helmer said. "I saw Sven Svenson Sunday afternoon. He said he'd been in Fosston and had been drunk, broke a big window, and got throwed in that shitty little two-cell jail. He wuz there when Charbeneau brung the kids in and dropt 'em in the other cell. They jist sat on the floor, all bloody, the girl rockin' the little one. He wuz whimperin' like a puppy and tryin' to wipe the blood off with his shirttail.

"Helga came in—you know, she's almost as tall as her boys and them Torgerson boys are over six feet. Sven said he'd never noticed her so tall before. With her hair hangin' all over her face, her clothes all tore up 'n bloody, she looked like hell warmed over."

"Hey, Fritz," Helmer said, "all this is makin' me mighty thirsty. How 'bout one on the house?"

"Hell, no. Go on with your story."

"Helga told Charbeneau that she wuz takin' her kids. Charbeneau said, 'Like hell you are. It's about time you Torgersons learn it ain't what you want, it's what I want. I'm the law and you and your big boys ain't. I hope you learned your lesson tonight. Go home.'

"Helga said, 'I'm not going without my kids.'

"Real ugly-like, Charbeneau said, 'I said you ain't taking them kids with you tonight.'

" 'Then I'll stay till my boys get here,' Helga told him.

"Sven said he got the shivers—her voice wuz colder than the river ice. Then he heard Charbeneau say, 'Take them—and get the hell out.'"

CHAPTER 2

Hidden away, like a dirty little secret, was this town named Obeege, pronounced "o-b-g" we were told, that was just a stone's throw from the Minnesota-Canada border. Population: three hundred.

The year was 1933 and the depression still lingered.

Scattered about as though tossed from the careless hand of an uncaring God were small farms and whiskey stills. Stills, buried deep in the dark veiled woods, gave additional income and happy time out to the farmers who eked out a bare existence. Farmers who watched the corn grow with one eye as the other watched for the revenuer.

The faltering economy was saved by the WPA and the excellent market in the big cities for the potent "white lightning"—the lifeline to the real world.

A broken stretch of sidewalk was declared to be "Main Street" by a sign wedged haphazardly in the fork of a tree. That sign introduced the small businesses huddled together as though seeking sanctuary from the blizzards that raged down from the Great Plains of Canada or perhaps the blazing summers that gave no quarter.

Haldor's Bar made itself known by the large sign that clung precariously to its faded front and, just below, as though an afterthought, the words "Fer Sale" painted in big black letters.

A nickelodeon could vaguely be seen through the window etched with frost at Sorenson's Pool Hall. Melby's Dry Goods Store doubled as a post office. Just across the muddy street, a one-pump gas station leaned against the shabby little office of the WPA.

At one end of town stood the Catholic church. At the other end, the Lutheran steeple stood proud. On the far corner was the schoolhouse, which housed grades one through twelve, although no one seemed to remember anyone who had ever made it through twelfth grade.

Beyond that, a grain elevator, deserted now, was starkly outlined against the sky like a giant exclamation point.

At the end of Main Street stood the town's largest building, an abandoned sheep shed converted to a public meeting place with rough-sawn plank floors, above which stood a small platform, and wooden benches along the walls. This building hosted the town's festivities—usually wedding dances on a Saturday night that continued through the weekend.

The town was almost evenly divided between the tall blond Norwegians and Swedes and the feisty, shorter French-Canadians, whose older generation still spoke their mother tongue and mangled the English language, as did the Norwegians not too long off the boat.

The undercurrent of animosity and prejudice hung strongly between the "Norskies" and the "Catlickers," and was frequently appeased by a no-holds-barred bare-knuckled bloody fight that terminated only when one enthusiast was unable to get to his feet.

Fighting and fornicating were the two recreational activities that made both priest and pastor despair.

Wedding dances, where moonshine flowed like a river, seemed to present the perfect opportunity to address all wrongs, both real and imaginary. But many of the younger generation strayed far beyond their parents' old-country customs. The fiery, aggressive Frenchmen, with their dark good looks, spontaneous laugh, and devil-may-care ways, melted the reserve of the fair-skinned Nordic maidens and swept them off their feet and into the hay with an amazing regularity.

After tears and recriminations, the parents would reluctantly consent to the marriage—usually the bride was at least three months pregnant, and the wedding dress was tight across her belly. Both parents lamented the fact that their offspring had muddied their gene pool.

CHAPTER 3

"Fritz, get up! It's almost noon! Don't just lay there and vegetate. Why don't you find something to do?"

I struggled to find my pants that seemingly had sought refuge under the bed. I dared not look for my shoes lest they had followed. But then, by sheer luck, my bleary eyes fastened on the chair upon which my pants hung. Dangling from a pocket by its golden chain was my watch.

I was delighted to know that I hadn't misplaced it again. This watch was a gift from the appreciative board members of the best high school in Minneapolis, where I had taught for twenty-five years. That was so long ago.

The fog suddenly cleared.

Is this all there is? I'm bored to death. I'm rotting away. I hate this retirement!

Those thoughts had been festering for months; now they climaxed.

"Bessie!" I bellowed. "I want to move. Somewhere I can fish and loaf and play stud poker with the good old boys.

Some quiet, beautiful hamlet where people are friendly. Far away from the problems and turmoil of the big city.

"Maybe you should go back to bed. You don't sound well."

The door slammed, only to reopen moments later.

"You're almost eighty, you know. Are you hallucinating? You know I'll never, ever move."

We moved to Obeege.

Looking back—remembering our first visit there in May— it was a balmy day that long-ago spring. The streets had dried up by then, and the mosquitos were still honing their skills in Canada.

"What a quaint little town," said Bessie.

"Yes, quaint," I agreed. "Exactly what we're looking for."

Time passed and I noticed the fish in Lost River had not been too anxious to make my acquaintance and the weather was cold.

Bessie's flowers had made her the scandal of the neighborhood because they dared to bloom when other ladies were harvesting their peas and carrots.

My fishing rod hung dusty in the woodshed, while I wandered about the house looking for anything to occupy my time. When Bessie yelled at me to find something—anything— to do, I hurriedly looked for something worth of my abilities.

I wandered down Main Street and stumbled upon a dilapidated, down-at-the-heels little bar. The crooked sign wore the words, "Haldor's Bar—Fer Sale."

This was my chance, I rejoiced! The timing was perfect—a golden opportunity to meet the locals, the real people! I bought it on the spot.

I imagined chatting with a favorite customer over a Sloe

Gin Fizz or a martini. Little did I realize that this bar did not attract that kind of clientele. A loud rap on the bar for a straight shot of corn whiskey, or better yet, moonshine with the clinging fragrance of the wood-fired mash still permeating the atmosphere and a hurry it up!

My illusions faded.

The town was slow to accept us since it was pretty much evenly divided between the Norwegians and the French-Canadians who had strayed over the border. We, of German ancestry, were the square pegs in the round holes of the not-yet-forgotten war with the Kaiser.

The first year it had been "quaint."

The following year it was "different."

Then came the grim reality.

The Torgersons had been our first friends in this closed little town. Helga became Bessie's best friend. The thought of that unspeakable brutality hung in my mind all day. I closed early and went home.

With my arms piled high with firewood, I pushed the door open with my foot and dropped the wood in the woodbox beside the old stove.

Bessie turned, her apron white with flour, a spatula in her hand.

"Thanks, honey, I knew it was getting low, but I've been busy making lefse all day—or trying to—between listening on the party line and worrying about the lefse burning. You've been hearing it all day too, I suppose?"

"Yes, it's been a long miserable day."

"Well, sit down and have a cup of coffee. The last piece of

lefse is hot on the stove—I saved it for you. Sugar or butter?"

"Both. Have you heard from Helga?"

"Yes. Said she took the kids right from the jail to the Thief River Falls hospital. Buddy, poor little boy, had a broken nose and, of course, his eyes are turning black too. He was always scared of the dark and now he has reason to be, I'd guess. He was Helga's change-of-life baby, you know, and she has always been embarrassed about that. Guess she didn't want anyone to know she and Ole were having sex at that age. I think she was in her forties."

"Yeah, but Ole would have been proud if he'd been alive." I smiled at the thought.

"What about the girl?"

"She had a concussion and got thirty stitches on one side of her head. The doctor had to shave a lot of hair off—that beautiful hair that she could almost sit on. Three ribs are taped, and she's bruised all over. When she got home, she took the scissors and cut the rest of her hair almost as short as a boy's."

Bessie's voice broke and I could almost hear the tears.

"She lay in bed and wouldn't talk, wouldn't eat. The boys were home by this time. Orren sat by her bed and cried like a baby. Can you believe that? Ila is that family's pride and joy."

"Boys? Bessie, they aren't boys. I wish people would get past that tag. Olaf is twenty-six. I know because I stood him a drink on his birthday. Orren is a few years younger."

Both boys are over six feet tall, and I'd guess they'd tip the scales at a hundred and eighty pounds of solid muscle—not an ounce of fat, and damned good to look at. They're either your friend or your enemy. There's no in-between. Hell,

I'd rather wrestle a grizzly bear. They're good men and take good care of the family and the farm. Sure, they've raised a little hell, but everybody in two counties knows not to mess with them.

"What's for supper? I'm starved."

"I'm working on it. Have another cup of coffee. What was Charbeneau so sore about anyhow?"

"Well, Bessie, I've heard some different stories so it depends on who you believe—the Frenchies or the Norwegians. But most agree it was over a boar that Charbeneau bragged was purebred and that he had the papers to prove it. The boar weighed over six hundred pounds and was as big as a yearling calf. Charbeneau even bragged he was meaner than hell. He complained he had paid all that money for the boar and still had to pay the freight bill. Bought him in Bemidji.

"Charbeneau said if the hogs were bred right, there was more money in hogs than whiskey stills. Bigger litters, bigger hogs, bigger money. Of course, that got everyone's attention."

I stepped over to the stove and lifted the lid from the skillet.

"Damn, that smells good. What are you cooking? I'm about to starve," I complained.

"Finish that story, Fritz. I think you'll live."

I poured myself a cup of coffee and sat back down.

"Olaf and Orren happened in and listened to his bragging. You know, they raise hogs like the rest of these farmers. They carried their drinks over where Charbeneau and his cronies were talking and asked if they could rent that boar for a month. Said they'd pay ten dollars.

" 'Hell, no,' said the Frenchman. 'Why should I do you Norskies a favor? I've got sixteen sows of my own to keep him busy for a couple of years, then I'll salt him down. I'll have some breeding stock for sale and then, maybe, just maybe, I'll sell you one if you've got enough money.'

"Olaf told Charbeneau that he'd give him fifteen dollars now, that he just needed that boar for a month. Charbeneau said, 'Hell, no. Keep your money. Go home and tell your mother to wipe your nose and maybe your ass too.'

"Of course, the Frenchies laughed as the Torgersons walked out. Somehow Charbeneau's barn burned to the ground a couple of weeks later. Nobody knows how that happened. The next week, his tires were about sliced off the rims. Charbeneau called Olaf and told him he'd reconsidered, to come and get the boar. So now he's got new tires and they're still on the rims....

"How long until supper? Will I have enough strength to lift a fork?"

"Hang on, it's almost done. You want to eat it raw?" Bessie pushed her hair back and snapped, "And stop nagging. Relax or you're going to wear it, okay? Go on with your story."

"Bessie," I said, "what are you so touchy about?"

Without waiting for a response, I sat down and continued. "Well, everything seemed quiet for a month, then Charbeneau wanted the boar back as agreed. Olaf said, 'Maybe it will be awhile. I've loaned that boar to a neighbor—just being neighborly, you know, then the farmer next door has borrowed him and he has neighbors too—so it might be awhile.'

"And 'awhile' it's been—almost four months, and Olaf has made it known that the boar is in pig heaven because he's made so many sows happy and there's more waiting.

"Olaf told Charbeneau, 'Maybe, just maybe, they could

talk about it when he and Orren got back from a fishing trip. Maybe.'

"Bessie, can you imagine how crazy mad that Frenchman was? He waited almost four months for the chance to get even and then, when the boys were gone, he took the kids.

"Bessie! Pork chops and home-grown taters! That root cellar sure keeps them good, doesn't it? Now I know why I married you. Pass the ketchup.

"Why so quiet, honey? You're crying—did I say something wrong? That was a compliment."

"I'm crying because those grown men are playing dirty pool and who gets hurt? Two kids. Two innocent kids beaten up and thrown in a dirty jail. Helga man-handled, dragged in the dirt, begging for her kids."

Bessie stomped her feet. "I hate this ugly town. We've never really fit in here. Can't we please, please, please! move back to civilization. You promised me years ago—how long is it going to take?"

CHAPTER 4

I opened the bar early today. Even so, when the door opened Helmer and his buddy hurried in.

"Are you two outlaws off the job again?" I demanded. "When are you going to get that water main in? Everybody's waiting; tired of that ditch being dug down Main Street right down the middle. Good thing the rest of the crew stays on the job."

My sarcasm didn't seem to register as I asked, "What will it be, gentlemen, a martini or a Chivas Royale?"

"The usual," Helmer replied with irritation.

"You shoulda stuck to teachin', yer so damn smart. Better make it a double for me 'n my sidekick. Pour 'em heavy."

"Helmer," I said, "you never give your sidekick the chance to say a word. Can't he talk for himself?"

"Nah, he's from North Dakota and them farmers don't talk much, so I get to do the tellin'."

He downed his drink with a gulp and settled back.

"Caught a ride in with Orren this morning. He wuz takin'

the cream to town and we got to talkin'. He said he wuz out doin' the chores last night jist before dark when he seen sumpthin moved in the snow, way down in the far pasture. He thought it might be a deer so he took his gun and went on down. But when he got close, he saw it wuz Charbeneau's woman, Marguerite. She wuz carryin' a kid and a little boy bawlin' his head off wuz hangin' on to her skirt. She wuz plowin' through snow way up to her knees."

"How did she get in that pasture?" I asked.

"I ast Orren the same question. He said that his pasture connects at the far end with Charbeneau's where he keeps his hogs. He told me the woman had cut across; it wuz about a mile and a half that way. It wuz jist gittin' dark and the milkin' wuzn't done, so Orren jist picked up the boy and brung her and the baby on up to the house.

"Helga wuz plum put out to see the shape they wuz in— 'bout froze and so hungry. Marguerite ate three bowls of soup and fell asleep at the table. Hard walkin' in the snow, I'd guess, carrying a three-year-old baby girl. Helga jist put them all to bed and slept with Ila, I spose."

Helmer stopped long enough to roll a cigarette and throw his match on the floor.

"In the mornin', Marguerite said she wuz jist comin' to ask the boys if they would look in on that boar. He hadn't been up to eat since they brung him home. Said Charbeneau would kill her if anything happened to that boar, but I'm thinkin' she's gettin' desperit 'cause she said she wuz out of firewood and had been burnin' anything she could find, and the kids had been out of milk for a week.

"That bastard—to light out and leave her with no money

and no wood for goin' on three weeks, ain't it?"

While I waited, Helmer stopped to relight his cigarette, then threw the match on the floor.

"Dammit, Helmer! Stop throwing your crap on the floor, will you? I just swept up."

"I'll bet when he gits back them Torgerson boys will learn him how to treat a woman and he'll learn fast if he lives through the lesson. Bet they're better teachers than you are, Fritz."

He looked at me and grinned, but I didn't take the bait.

"The boys went over and looked at the boar and told her not to worry. He wuz jist fine, but plum tuckered out, they said, and laughed fit to bust.

"Orren took Marguerite to Melby's to get some groceries, on credit, of course. Olaf brung her some wood and stacked it on the porch. She wuz cryin' on the way to town, said she wuz scart of them pigs, 'specially that big boar. She had reason to be—who wuzn't scart of him! So Orren told her if she'd stop cryin', he'd take care of them hogs for her.

"You know Orren, he never wuz one to miss a chance to comfort a pretty woman and she sure is a pretty one. Big brown eyes and even after two kids, she's got a figger that puts most girls to shame," he laughed.

"I can't help thinkin'," he said, looking thoughtful, "three days after Charbeneau leaves, they bring that boar back."

"Maybe they talked it over and just decided to be neighborly," I suggested.

"With Charbeneau? I doubt it."

"Now will you get out of here and get to work?"

"Wait a minute—wait! Don'tcha know it's bad manners to

interrupt? I wuz jist gittin' to the good part.

"Helga said she couldn't sleep nights for thinkin' about that Charbeneau woman and her kids—all sleepin' in one bed tryin' to keep warm, and most likely hungry too, so Helga jist sent the boys over to bring her and the kids home.

"Now it seems like they jist melted into the Torgerson family like butter on a hotcake. Helga actin' like they're her own flesh 'n blood. Ain't that sumpthin?"

CHAPTER 5

The next day I was finishing up a few chores, thinking I'd go home a little early, when Helmer banged in. I hoped that storm door would hold together till spring.

"Yeah, I'm late, but I been puttin' in a little time with the WPA crew," he grinned. "Doesn't that make you happy? You otta stand me a drink for that sacrifice. No? Guess not. I'm goin' out to the Torgersons to show them boys how to fix a well casing without pullin' the damn thing out. Helga will probably invite me to stay for supper and if she smells likker on me, the chances are slim."

"How the hell do you know so much about the Torgersons?" I asked. "You kissing cousins or something?"

"Guess you haven't been here long enough to know, Fritz. Twenty-five, mebbe thirty years ago, Helga had to pick between me 'n Ole. Course, he got home from the war a few months before me and then too, he had his pa's big farm. Near broke my heart—that's when I took to drinkin'. Weren't never any woman fer me but Helga.

"I helped out there after Ole died—kinda like family, ya know. I love them kids—the boys call me 'Unk.' Helga and me have a cuppa coffee sometimes."

"Now that I've heard the story of your life, will you get the hell out of here so I can get home early for a change? And you better be on time in the morning. Don't forget your shovel or your Uncle Sam is going to fire you and then I'm going to get stuck with your tab, which is beginning to look like the national war debt. Now get!"

"Okay, okay, I'm leavin'. I've been thinkin' about that boar. I just keep thinkin' why them boys brung him back three days after they got home. Gave Marguerite the $15 jist as perlite. I jist can't put it out of my mind...."

"Helmer!"

"Okay, okay. Olaf ast where do you want him and she said, 'Put him down in the far pen behind the feed shed. I don't wanta look at him. I sure don't blame her—he is an ugly son of a bitch. Don't know what their hurry wuz after holdin' on to him almost four months. Hell, I'm surprised they even brung him back. You know, all kinds of accidents can happen on a farm. That damn boar could even have died of pneumonia," he grinned.

"Helmer, will you please go home? I want to leave early!"

"All right, all right. Don't git so hot. Like I wuz sayin', I can't help thinkin'.... Huh? Jist put it on the tab, will ya. Say Fritz, did I tell you that Marguerite went to work at Melby's store, payin' off her grocery bill at twenty cents an hour? Worse than the WPA.

"Fritz, did I tell you.... Wait a minute, yer always in such a damn hurry to go home. I stopt in at Sorenson's this morning 'cause you wuz late openin' up again. Them farmers were standin' around spittin' Copenhagen and shootin' pool, layin' bets as to whose sow wuz gonna have the biggest litter. Turns out Torgersons next-door neighbor won the pot—his sow had fifteen. Now them farmers are countin' on big money and it's lookin' good. That boar wuz worth the money."

"Hope his progeny don't inherit his disposition."

"There you go agin, Perfesser, usin' them big words. Who cares about stuff like that when yer chompin' down on a pork roast cooked jist right or even pickled pigs' feet?"

"Helmer, if you don't get the hell out of here so I can lock up…."

"All right, all right. I'll be takin' my business to Sorenson's. At least he opens on time."

CHAPTER 6

As I hurried down to the bar, I could see my breath—it almost seemed to freeze in the air. I had hardly closed the door behind me when Helmer slammed in.

"Dammit to hell! Don't tear in here like a maniac. You just fixed that hinge—now you've probably screwed it up again. What in the world is going on with you?"

"Yer late again, Perfesser. Is that any way to run a business? I want to get out of this cold drizzle, that's what's goin' on with me, you stingy old crank. Isn't it supposed to be springtime soon? Hey! I've got headline news—not an hour old—that I'll trade for a good stiff drink. How about it, Fritz?"

"Maybe," I answered, "but it better be good. Isn't it payday for you WPA guys? I'd better see some of it on your tab. What's on your mind?"

I almost laughed out loud to hear his triumphant voice as though the WPA had mistakenly overpaid him.

"I know where Charbeneau is, and he ain't comin' back. Start pourin'! Marguerite got a letter with a St. Paul postmark. No return address. His wedding ring wuz in it. Ain't that as good as a divorce? Them young bucks hangin' 'round will be waitin' in line, but I think Orren's got the lead."

"That's none of our business. What did Marguerite say? I ought to have all the details for that drink I poured. I poured a double, you know."

Helmer looked hopeful at the bottle, then down at his suddenly empty glass. I ignored it.

"Well, all the WPA crew wuz crowded in that little corner of Melby's where the post office is, waitin' for the mail truck. Everybody happy, jokin', laughin'. Payday comes only once a month, you know. Thirty big ones—that's money them farmers ain't seen for a while. Marguerite wuz behind the counter keepin' busy. You know she's been workin' there to pay off her grocery bill."

He tapped his glass, but I shook my head. He looked disgusted.

"You know, Helga has been keepin' the kids. Frankie— that's the boy's name. He's Charbeneau's son, you know. Same age almost as Buddy and, of course, the little girl. 'Baby Doll,' they call her."

"Helmer, I don't want a genealogy lesson. Get on with it."

"Well, Miz Melby wuz in the back. We could smell the soup cookin'. You know how she always keeps a big pot on the stove. Costs twenty cents for a big bowl and a hunka bread."

"Helmer," I said, "I'm really not interested in her menu. Get to the information I've already paid you for."

"Keep yer shirt on or you'll make me fergit. As I wuz sayin', everybody wuz havin' a good time."

"Well, you happy people better remember me on your payday and put something on the tab so I can be happy too."

"Fritz, if yer gonna keep breakin' in like this, you kin jist set the bottle over here. As I wuz sayin', the truck finally pulled up and we could hear the mailman stuffin' the boxes when he called, 'Anybody here name of Charbeneau? Package too big fer the box. A letter too.'

"Marguerite stepped around the counter and said, 'Ah, my Sears and Roebuck catalog…and a letter for me?'

"Then everybody wuz diggin' in their own boxes when they heard this awful screech like a cat with its tail caught in the door…"

He reached for the bottle, but I snatched it away. I heard him cussing under his breath.

"Yeah, she wuz screechin' and everybody turned to look. We saw the package on the floor and Marguerite laughin' and cryin', with one hand holdin' the envelope. In the other she wuz holdin'…holdin' sumthin between her fingers. Turned out to be Charbeneau's wedding ring. Her voice wuz all choked— she had to say 'wedding ring' a coupla times to get the words out. Miz Melby hurried and tried to put her arms around the pore thing, but Marguerite jist pushed her way and laughed like I never heard before, and then she throwed that ring so hard and so fast it bounced off the cash register and plum disappeared into a shelf of canned peaches. She tore off her apron and lit out the door headed to the Torgersons. All we could hear wuz her yellin' 'Thank God, thank God,' and she wuz laughin' like she wuz plum crazy. Don't that beat all?"

I poured him a short one.

CHAPTER 7

I had just put away most of a pot roast and Bessie was chattering like a magpie.

"Well, it is a joy to see the pink and purple crocus showing above the muddy snow. Don't know how they survive these frigid winters. You'll remember you promised me we'd be out of here before the next one. When are you going to put up the for sale signs? You do remember, of course."

I could feel this conversation was leading up to something I wanted to forget.

"Well, Bessie, I can't say I do remember. Was that an exact promise? You know, I'm doing better now and I can't sell in the summer—that's when I would make the most profit—so it might take a year or two."

I reached for her, but she slapped my hand away.

"Fritz! Look at me! I can't believe you're not going to keep your word. You promised, you know you did."

Her face flushed red and that was always a bad sign.

"Bessie, Bessie, keep your voice down. Did I put my hand

on the bible? Circumstances change, you know. My business has picked up, the town is growing and improving."

I tried without success to explain my perfectly reasonable decision.

" 'Circumstances' be damned. Your wife—that's me—hasn't changed, and I expect you to keep your word."

"Well, I may have indicated that perhaps we might move, sometime, but now I believe we'll just stay put. Summers are when I show a profit. Don't look like that!"

"You're reneging, and I won't spend another winter here. You've got until October to get these properties sold, and then I'm moving. Maybe your 'profit' will keep your belly full and your bed warm."

"Those are mighty strong words, Bessie. Don't threaten me—I'll do what I think is best for us."

"Don't count on it. I'll do what is best for me, and you can take that to the bank with your 'profit.'"

I tried to assert myself as master of the house. "The subject is closed, Bessie. I'll hear no more of it. What's for supper?"

"I don't know Melby's exact menu, but I believe it's soup. I want the car keys, I'm going out."

"You know I don't want you out at night in my car, Bessie."

"I believe it's our car, and I promise you I'll only drive my half."

"Bessie!" I exclaimed, but handed over the keys.

Days later I entreated. "Bessie, I've eaten at Melby's so many times that people are starting to talk."

"They will probably talk more about the nice man who walked me home from the store. Some friend of yours, I believe."

"What will people say? Are you trying to shame me, Bessie?"

"How can I shame you? You've shamed yourself. A man who breaks his word isn't much of a man."

"Can I help it if you misunderstood me? When are you going to cook something I can chew on?"

"As soon as the for sale signs go up…maybe. I'm really enjoying my extra time now that I'm not stuck in front of that cookstove. I saw Orren putting up some for sale signs for Marguerite's pigs. He sure is a handsome devil. No wonder the girls fall for him. Yes, he surely is a handsome man and a sweet-talker too. I wonder how he would take to a mature woman."

"Bessie! What in hell is happening to you?"

"Nothing. That's why I wondered."

The door slammed and Helmer barged in.

"Hey, Fritz. How ya doin'? Jist ran into town fer some nails. Got a cuppa coffee? Saw yer wife in Melby's. How did you manage to git such a young one? She's a fine figger of a woman, friendly too. I walked her home, carried her groceries. She don't look very strong, real delicate like, not the draft horse type—more like a pretty little pony. You know, the kind you like to pet…

"Look it, Fritz! You've spilt that coffee all over the bar. Are you nervous or sumpthin?"

"My wife is the same age as I am, and she's strong enough to carry her own groceries. I take good care of all the petting— got that?"

"Well—well—Fritz! Well, I never. I wuz jist bein' friendly—neighborlike...."

"Be neighborly with somebody else's wife."

"I'm leavin'. Guess I'll jist take my business to Sorenson's. I didn't know you wuz the jealous kind. Better git this coffee off the bar 'for it eats the shine off, and don't be thinkin' about puttin' that on my tab. I'm leavin' now."

He stomped off and slammed the door.

Then I was ashamed of myself that I had let him aggravate me, and more than a little. I was aggravated at Bessie too. Everyone will be talking.

I felt the glass break and saw the blood on the bar towel. Damn! I dried that glass with a little too much enthusiasm.

I had just finished cleaning up that mess when Helmer stormed back in and announced, "Jist met the new pastor and we had a little talk. Believe me, he's all hellfire and brimstone and he won't be takin' any sass. Probably be lookin' in on you."

Damn! There went another glass. The door banged shut, again.

CHAPTER 8

"Bessie, I'm home. something sure smells good. Is that pot pie?"

We both knew I was lying, but I thought I could ignite the cooking spark and hoped she might have come around to my way of thinking. She is an intelligent woman, I rationalized, and by now she should have figured out that I was the one to make the decisions. Of course she would see it my way, and, damn, I was tired of Mrs. Melby's soup.

I opened the oven, but it was empty. The table wasn't even set. I looked over my shoulder and saw Bessie with her hands on her hips.

"Have the for sale signs gone up yet?"

That soft tone of voice didn't fool me; I knew I was walking through a minefield.

I squared off, disregarding the little voice in the back of my mind that told me if those signs didn't go up I was going to make Mrs. Melby's soup a national delicacy.

The thought of Bessie's pot pie strengthened me, but I

don't know why my voice sounded so weak.

"Bessie, you know we've discussed that and…"

"Good-night, Fritz."

She closed the door behind her, the spare bedroom door. Our bedroom seemed as empty as the Sahara Desert. It had been almost four weeks and three days that I'd been going down to the bar early and making a pot of coffee since Bessie wasn't making breakfast anymore.

Three days later, I flew the white flag of surrender. The last of my pride had dissipated and I was hungry. Hungry for the loving relationship that had been ours for fifty years, and, perhaps, errant thoughts of apple pie and pot roast may have come to mind.

"Bessie, I think I've got an ulcer now. Too much of Mrs. Melby's soup has ruined my digestive system. You've damn near broken my heart by sleeping in the spare bedroom. You've got me on my knees. Is that where you want me?"

"I don't want a man on his knees, I want a man who stands behind his word."

"Well, Bessie, I'm standing. Should have done it long before this. Pride is a poor bedfellow. I want it like it was before, so I'll put the signs up. It's only April—hopefully it will sell before October. If it doesn't, I'll board it up. Over fifty years we've been together, Bessie. I love you."

"Oh Fritz, that's what I want to hear. To know you love me more than this real estate. I love you, love you—you're the only man in the world for me. Pull the shades down and let's rest awhile. Your ulcer, you know."

"Bessie, you know I can't sleep in the daytime."

"Yes, I know.

"Fritz, put me down! Don't blow in my ear."

"I'm not blowing, I'm whispering."

"Well, it gives me goosebumps. How can you say such wicked things? Stop! This is intensely inappropriate for people of our age. We're seventy years old, for goodness sake. Mrs. Melby says sex for pleasure is a sin—it's just an animal instinct."

"Woof-woof! C'mon, Bessie. I'll show you seventy is just a number."

"Fritz, supper is getting cold."

"Hellfire! Do I care? It's getting damned hot under these covers."

"Oooh, Fritz. Fritz, oh…"

"C'mon, c'mon, Helmer, get with it. I want to go home. My wife will be getting impatient."

"Wish I had a wife to go home to. What's her name agin?"

"Bessie." *Bessie, my Bessie.* "What the hell are you laughing about?"

"Yer lookin' all starry-eyed, Perfesser, that's what."

"Why don't you go on home, Helmer. I'm not discussing my wife."

"Well I spose that's reasonable if she's bucktoothed and bowlegged."

"Damn you, Helmer. I ought to kick your sorry ass out of here."

"There must be sumpthin you don't wanta say—can't she cook?"

"For your information, she's the best cook this side of the Rockies."

"I'd guess Helga Torgerson might doubt that brag."

"Well, I'm not talking to you about my wife. Go home now."

"Well, there must be sumpthin yer hidin' if you can't talk about it."

"If I wanted to talk about it, I'd say she has the same beautiful legs she had fifty years ago and her teeth are her own."

"Maybe she's carryin' a little too much weight, Fritz?"

"Hell, no! She might be a few pounds heavier than she was fifty years ago, but, believe me, it still jiggles in all the right places when she walks. She's a little dumpling—good enough to bite."

"Bite? Fritz—bite? Why would you bite? You otta be ashamed of yerself, talkin' dirty about yer wife. I'm leavin' now."

In a rage, I locked the door behind him and hurried home.

A week later, I was sweeping up the floor down at the bar when Helmer stumbled in.

"Hi Fritz. Are you over yer temper? How ya doin'? I think I'm comin' down with the flu. Don't feel too good. Went up to Bjournsons yestidday to see about talkin' him out of some settin' hens. A weasel got all of mine. Well, we got to talkin' and he poured me a coupla shots of that white lightnin' he's been makin' in that still he's got hid up there in the brush. Then, to be perlite, I had a few more an' that rotgut near killed me. Ya got any black coffee back there? I woulda stopped at Helga's, but I know she's busy with Marguerite's kids. Think she's 'bout adopted that woman. Playin' grandma to them little ones. They're all crazy 'bout that baby girl. She's pretty as a picher with them big brown eyes and curly hair. Dimples too. Looks just like her ma.

"Helga says Olaf doesn't look so tough playin' patty-cake with that three-year-old baby or when he's carryin' her piggyback. Ain't that sumpthin?

"Oooh, man, I ain't never gonna drink that homemade hooch again. I think I'm gonna die. Is there another cup in that pot?"

"Well, you're still able to talk, so I think you'll live," I said without much sympathy.

"Yer all heart, Perfesser. I'd pour, but my hands 'er shakin' like I wuz wavin' goodbye. Mebbe I got frostbite. Lost my mittens up there in the brush. I b'lieve this April is jist as cold as February. One more cup, Fritz, 'n then I'll try fer home."

"Did I hear you say goodbye? That's a great idea. Sorry this isn't a home for wayward drunks. Don't puke on my clean floor." I hurried for the pail.

"That's all right, Perfesser, no need to apologize. You done the best you could."

"Dammit to hell, will you put it in the pail? In the pail!"

CHAPTER 9

"You're late this morning, Fritz. Sleeping in?"

"Yeah, I've been neglecting my wife so she says, so we dawdled over breakfast." It seemed to me that the fragrance of her perfume lingered in my every pore. I stepped back and asked, "What's up, Olaf?"

"I'm looking for Helmer. Haven't seen him for a couple of days. Have you?"

"He was in two or three days ago, I think. Drunk and sick. Puked all over my clean floor. Said he was going home. He's killing himself with that rotgut whiskey, that homemade poison that Bjournson's cooking. He comes by mostly to shoot the bull. Can't help but like him, but wish he would straighten up. Doesn't he have any family?"

"Guess you didn't know he'd been found on the Halverson's doorstep early one morning. Musta been about fifty years ago. He was naked, wrapt in a cotton blanket covered with snow and about froze. The Halversons were a middle-aged couple who never had kids and sure didn't want any, so they took him to town. Nobody would claim him.

"The Norwegians said he must belong to the French because he had black hair. The Frenchies said he didn't look like any of their kin so he must be an Indian—there were lots of them in those days. But this black-haired, dark-skinned baby had funny blue eyes."

"What's so unusual about blue eyes?" I interrupted. "Hell, yours are the same funny color—sometimes they look almost black."

"Yeah, Ma calls it navy blue. One of the old-timers said there was a part of Norway where they all had that coloring."

"And still nobody would take him?"

"Nah. Of course, everybody had big families then. Hell, who needed another mouth to feed? Dad's sister had eight boys and three girls and raised nine of them. Two of the girls died from whooping cough."

"Well, what happened to this baby?"

"The priest was going to put him in an orphanage, but after a couple of weeks, Mrs. Halverson wouldn't give him up. She raised him on goats' milk and love, I guess. He went to the same school Dad did through sixth grade, then quit to work on the farm. He joined the army when he was seventeen and got leave to come home once to bury his ma. Then was sent overseas to fight the Kaiser."

"Don't point at me, Olaf. We weren't related. Anyhow, I'm trying to pass for a Swede."

"Good luck! You look like a Kraut to me."

"Lucky for you, I know you're joking. Go on with your story."

"Dad joined later and somehow they met up over there

and became best buddies. He said Helmer was a top gunnery sergeant and his men would have followed him anywhere. He got some medals, two for bravery. His dad brought them to town and bragged, he was so proud."

"That's a helluva story, Olaf."

"Yeah, then the war was over and Helmer came home. His dad was at the end and Helmer took care of him until he died. Spent every cent of his savings on the fancy casket and the gravestone. Still out there in the old cemetery that's covered with weeds. All but Helmer's folks—he keeps them nice. He still lives in the old shack on that Godforsaken forty acres, raises whatever he can just enough to live, and works for anyone who needs a hired hand.

"Don't know how we would have made it without him when Dad died. He wouldn't take a penny, either. Yeah, he and Dad were close. Ma has pictures of them in uniform, holding a bottle, arms around each other. Helmer was a mighty handsome man, whatever his blood. I think he was sweet on Ma, but Dad got home first and Helmer just drifted. He's still family.

"Wonder where in hell he got to. I'll drive out to see if he's sick or just sleeping it off. See you later, Fritz."

I watched him drive off and thought that Helmer was a lucky man to have the Torgersons in his corner.

CHAPTER 10

Helmer hadn't come in for weeks. I asked some of my regulars if they had seen him, but no one had. Then, one cold, snowy morning, he showed up.

"Hey, damned if it ain't Helmer! You've been gone so long I've almost missed you. What's it been—a month? Olaf was in, said you'd been sick."

"Sick? I durn near cashed it in and you'd never got that tab paid where I wuz headin'. Bjournson's rotgut 'bout poisoned me. I laid up there in that cold cabin too sick to build a fire and woulda froze 'cept Olaf came by. I jist don't remember how he carried me back and put me in the bunkhouse and built a big fire.

"Every time I woke up Orren and Olaf wuz there. I wuz trying to run out in the snow it wuz so sweatin' hot. Them shakes and crawly things came right out of the ceilings and the walls—guess the heat musta brung 'em out and them spiders wuz bigger'n chickens. Orren told me they wuzn't real, but I knowed he lied.

"Seems like Helga wuz there for a while, and then I wuz talkin' to God and I told him I'd do different if He gave me some time. When I woke up I seen Helga bring some of Ole's clothes down. She said that a decent man wore these and not to shame him. I guess she's kept them all these years. The boys had burnt all of mine and 'bout scrubbed all the skin offa me—Helga got what they missed. I never had such a rough talkin' to in my life.

"I tried to tell her it wuz Bjournson's fault, but she told me to leave that man alone, that it wuz God trying to get my attention, that I wuzn't too old to change. Then she said, 'Straighten up and be the man you once were. Stop being the town drunk.' I tried to get a word in, but she wuz lookin' fierce and talkin' fast so I promised her and I promised God no more boozin' for me ever. I'm a different man. So don't try pushin' any of them fancy martinis or Chivas Royal off on me anymore. If God don't get me, Helga will."

He almost danced out the door, waving a joyful goodbye.

Three days later, he danced back in. His happiness was contagious, especially since he said he was going to square his tab.

"Hey, Helmer, you back?"

"Hi, Fritz, it's a happy day for both of us. I quit the WPA, got my last check, and I'm gonna pay my tab. Set 'em up fer the crowd. I'm buyin'."

"What crowd? There's only the two of us."

"Well, hell, when's a better time? Two cups, make mine black. I'll add the sugar. Olaf's hired me to help Orren. That Orren! Always off courtin' so we're gettin' behind now. It's a big farm with plenty to do. I help Helga in the garden too.

Fifteen dollars a month, room 'n board, the bunkhouse is warm 'n clean. Helga even put curtains to the window, and I ain't never et so good. Seems like Orren has more time for courtin' now that them pigs are sold. You didn't hear about that? Coupla farmers bought 'em on shares. Marguerite got paid good—them sows were ready to farrow. Too bad about the boar, nobody wanted him—why would they? He'd bred every sow in two counties. After the sows went, that mean SOB rooted everything, plowed up about an acre with that snout, then attacked the wooden fence Orren put up. Got his head stuck sideways and jist hung hisself. Six hundred pounds of salt pork gone to waste.

"Helga really pushed Marguerite to stay the winter. I know she felt sorry for her—didn't seem like anyone else did. 'Charbeneau's wife,' you know how that goes. I don't think her and them kids woulda made it through the winter.

"Helga just told her to bring some clothes and move over. I think Helga figgered Buddy needed some help—poor little kid. He just hid in his room and didn't talk, hardly ate, got so skinny. When Frankie came—he's about a year younger than Buddy—and took up with the toys, Buddy just watched.

"But when Frankie threw a leg over Buster, the stick horse, the boys made a quick connection. Now they're like brothers—you seen one, you seen 'em both. The little devils are into everything. Helga gets after 'em with the wooden spoon. Buddy's nose has healed nice and straight.

"And that baby girl—she is everybody's baby doll. That's what Helga and Olaf call her. The boys call her 'Dolly.' You should see how she follows Olaf around, her baby steps tryin' to keep up, and then he scoops her up and she rides on his shoulders, every dimple showin', every curl bouncin'.

"Ila seems like a young lady—almost. Her hair has growed out a lot. Svenson's boy comes over every Sadidday night. I think there's things they'd rather be doin' than playin' cards with Helga and me.

"Don't know what happened with Orren and Marguerite— thought that wuz a go fer sure. He's off courtin' the new minister's daughter, I heard, and the pastor isn't much pleased. You know Orren—'Love 'em and leave 'em.'

"It's a happy family and I thank God I'm part of it."

I was thinking about that as I walked home. I liked Helmer. I sensed his potential, but it seemed to me that he could have done better. My call to judgment—he gave up too easy and for what?

"Bessie, I'm home. What good thing are you fixing?"

"Actually, I'm not fixing much tonight—it's leftovers. I put it all in a good stew and it's on the stove. Why don't you get a bowl and help yourself. You know where the bread is. I'm really tired—had a big day. Helga, Marguerite, and I went to Thief River Falls for a shopping spree and had a wonderful time. Lunched at the River Inn—a little pricy, but what wonderful desserts.

"Thought you said something about a cream pie last night."

"Did plan to, honey, but didn't have the time. We got a late start. It was Marguerite's day off and, now that she got those hogs sold, she's got a little money and wanted to buy some decent clothes. She has looked a little ragged, you know. I can always find something I need and Helga was shopping for Buddy."

"How come you got a late start, Bessie?"

"Well, that's a different story. I thought for a while we weren't going at all. Helga was so quiet—upset, really. Guess Marguerite has been talking about leaving for Quebec—said the bank had sent her a foreclosure notice. She hadn't known Charbeneau had mortgaged the farm to the hilt. She cried and said, 'They can have it. I've never had any happiness there.' Then Helga cried and you know she's not the crying kind, and said 'You've been like a daughter to me. You don't know that I lost a baby girl twenty-three years ago and nothing has ever filled that hole in my heart until you and the kids, and you can't know how I love those kids. I had hoped something was happening with you and Orren.' She was sobbing.

"Marguerite dropped to her knees and put her head in Helga's lap and cried. Then she said 'Something almost did happen when he brought me home from the dance on Saturday night. He put his arms around me and somehow my arms were around him. He felt so good against me and I thought he could never be close enough.'

"Helga had stopped crying and her hands were stroking Marguerite's hair as she listened.

" 'His kisses burned me everywhere his lips touched. I never wanted them to stop, but when I felt his hand beneath my dress, his fingers on my bare skin, as suddenly as my desire came, just as suddenly it drained away. I pushed his hands back. I knew it wasn't him I wanted.' "

"Great day, Bessie! Do I need to hear this?"

"Fritz, I felt like an eavesdropper. I didn't know what do, so I made a pot of coffee—it's still on the stove. They didn't seem to know I was there. Marguerite cried like her heart would break. Helga held her as Marguerite continued. 'I'm sorry, Orren,' she said. Then he asked, 'You don't love me?' 'Yes, I love you,' she said, 'like a brother. And that isn't enough.' He took it like a gentleman and asked 'Are you sure? My life is ruined.' 'I'm sure,' she told him. He buttoned up and walked her to the door.

"With tears streaming, Marguerite looked up. 'Oh, Helga, what is wrong with me?'

" 'Nothing is wrong with you. He wasn't the right one. It's Olaf, isn't it?'

" 'Yes, and he doesn't even know I'm alive.'

" 'Then we'll have to bring it to his attention. Dry your eyes and I'll dry mine. We're going shopping.'

"Fritz, we had a wonderful time. I bought two pairs of shoes and a darling hat and, believe me, Marguerite won't look ragged again. I've never seen Helga so happy."

"Well, Bessie, I've had an interesting day too. I think I got the jump on the party line—that's a real achievement, wouldn't you say?"

"Really, Fritz, what could that possibly be?"

"Well, Orren was in today, all jokes and laughing. Seems he deserted Marguerite for the new pastor's pretty blond daughter. Says she's a real knockout. Daddy is really strict—a hellfire and brimstone preacher—but she's pulling at the reins. You know Orren—that daddy won't be the first one Orren has outmaneuvered. But I feel sorry for Marguerite, being dumped like that."

"Well, don't be. I got the other half of your newsflash, Fritz. Don't waste your sympathy on Marguerite—she's got other plans."

CHAPTER 11

As I walked to the bar today, it seemed like miles. I'm tired even before I start out. "Woof-woof" three times a week may be an extravagance I can't afford. With Bessie sleeping in this morning, I haven't even had coffee and that makes me cranky.

"Damn you, Helmer! How many times have I told you not to slam that storm door? It's hanging by one hinge now. See that? One hinge!"

"Don't you be cussin' me, Fritz, or I'm comin' over this bar and learn you some manners."

"Who's going to lift you over the bar, old man?"

"Old man? Hell, yer twenty years older'n I am. Guess yer safe—I'd be ashamed to hurt a helpless seventy-year-old man."

"How do you know how old I am, big mouth?"

"I know lotsa things, big shot. You'd be surprised."

"Yeah, how long have I been married?"

"Fifty some years, and I know yer wife and some French wimmin 'bout mixed it up down at Melby's yestidday and…."

"How in hell…?"

"Yeah, yer wife wuz at the counter and some French woman pushed ahead and elbowed her and Mrs. Melby said yer wife elbowed her back and then some other Frenchies crowded her. Mrs. Melby told them they better watch their manners and go home or they'd be buyin' their groceries in Thief River Falls and that's thirty-five miles on a bad road."

Helmer started digging around in his pants, looking for cigarette papers.

"When are we gonna do something about them Frenchies? They got the jump on us when they voted Charbeneau in. Where the hell were we? What has he ever done for this dirty, ugly town? Lookit the streets, the schoolhouse is fallin' down, and I keep seein' Helga on the ground and hear the kids screamin' and nobody raised a hand. What is happenin' here?" He added with satisfaction, "I'm waitin' for Charbeneau to come back. The least he'll get off with is a horsewhippin' and the priest better be there to give him the last rites, the bastard."

I said, "Well, we can agree on that. Do wish we could get this town cleaned up. I could list a dozen things that should be done and we wouldn't need to be ashamed to live here."

"Let's start now, Fritz—now! Charbeneau has been gone a month. Let's surprise him when he discovers his key won't fit the lock anymore. Of course, Olaf is the man for the job. Now—now is the time."

"Helmer, sometimes you surprise me. That's a damned good idea. Can you put the word out? We'll have our own election—forget the Frenchies. They had their turn." I got caught up in my own rhetoric.

"We can meet here. How about Saturday night? Sounds

good to me. About time. I'll even stand the men a drink, and I'll bet tomorrow we'll have voted in a new sheriff and this town will be started on a different road. Who knows, someday you might be the mayor. Let's drink to it."

"Now that's another good idea," Helmer said. "I'll put the word out. And for your information, I didn't slam the door. Wuz the wind that done it." And the door closed with a bang.

My steps lengthened as I hurried home, anxious to share the news with Bessie.

"Oh, Fritz, how wonderful." Then she echoed Helmer's words, "About time. I won't breathe a word, I promise. Saturday night? I can hardly wait. Can I come?"

"No, no, of course not. It's men's work."

With my excitement growing, I rushed through supper, burning my mouth on the hot coffee, spilling the cream, and hurried back to find Helmer waiting.

"Fritz, we better bring up another case. We're gonna have a crowd."

And what a crowd it was.

The men drifted in by twos and threes in their heavy winter clothes that smelled of sweat and barn. I think every farmer in the county crowded in.

Conversations, low and ominous, hummed like a giant piece of machinery through hazy cigarette smoke, quiet curses, and shuffling feet.

Thoughts of Charbeneau's brutality hung in the air, raw and volatile.

A frightening thought came to me with sudden clarity: that one misspoken word could be the match that would ignite this crowd. I prayed that Olaf would find the right words to control the meeting and avoid disaster.

Suddenly Helmer was at my elbow with a declaration that comforted me.

"Fritz, this crowd could get ugly. One drink is all I've poured, and I've locked the door."

I could have kissed him.

I moved to the front and announced, "Men, this is a serious business meeting. I'm sure Helmer has given you the details. We need to be sober—there'll be drinks on the house after the vote. If there is anyone here who doesn't know Olaf Torgerson, I'd like to introduce him now and ask you to vote him in as our first sheriff."

I called him from the back of the room.

At that moment, there was a sharp knock at the door and I thought my heart would stop. Oh, no. Surely we weren't going to have a brawl with those Frenchies now. With hands that shook, I opened the door.

We were shocked into silence as Helga and Bessie swept in, followed by the women of the Lutheran Ladies' Aid Society.

Wordless, I could only stare.

I could almost feel the disbelieving murmur that swept through the room like an incoming tide. The men quieted and stirred uneasily, amazed by the women's entrance into a man's domain, a place where "good women" didn't cross the threshold.

Bessie—my Bessie—stepped forward and said, "We are here to tell you what we women want and what we will vote to get. May we sit down?"

Chairs appeared as if by magic, and the women sat.

Olaf's opening statements were short and to the point.

Then he said, "Let me see a show of hands of everyone who is satisfied with this town."

A moment passed. Not a hand was raised.

"If you people would give me the authority," Olaf continued, "this is what I would do. First, I would appoint a town council to establish the rules and regulations of law and order that this town so desperately needs and then deputize good men to enforce those laws. Men from both sides of the fence—both Norwegian and French—working together for the common good. This town cannot limp ahead on one leg—we must unite."

For a long moment, when I didn't dare breathe, a smothering quiet wrapped around the outraged men. Then the muttering and cursing deepened into the roar of a coming tornado as this radical statement took root.

I saw Orren appear from nowhere and stand beside his brother and was amazed to see Helmer on the other side. I banged the bar with my broom handle. Turning, I saw the sudden silence was not brought about by my effort, but by a young woman who stood to face the men while holding up a young child. She demanded, "Do you want your children, your grandchildren, to grow up in a town where the streets are a war zone? Where the rats breed like flies, where the gutters run full…" Her voice faltered, then Helga stood beside her.

The men's mumbled outrage at Olaf's unimaginable solution tapered to a whisper.

Helga, tall and elegant, spoke without hesitation of the women's needs and wants. "We mothers want something better, not only for our children, but for all of us. We deserve better. We are tired and discouraged with the drunken brawling, the dirt, and the pitiful excuse of a building we dare to call a school."

Another woman stood, and then another, until they stood as one. "We need new books, supplies, safe playground equipment, clean streets, some law and order…."

Their words came fast and determined and left no doubt in anyone's mind of their determination to make a change.

They concluded with "We want peace—peace! Enough fighting and bloodshed. Peace!" The words seemed to echo off the walls.

"We thank you for your time."

The women walked sedately to the door where the young woman turned and said, "Any man who won't give this his full support may be making his own oatmeal and sleeping in a cold bed."

Damned if those women didn't yell, "Amen, Sister!"

Helmer closed the door behind them and wiped his sweaty face on the back of his sleeve.

I looked at Olaf and saw a grin tugging at the corners of his lips.

Looking around the room, I saw the expressions on the men's faces and knew that the tide had turned.

The women had made a deep impression that had diffused the mounting anger, and now the men were reassessing their first response to Olaf's urge to unite the warring populace.

Then the pros and cons waged without mercy until the wee small hours when we were all exhausted.

I rapped on the bar.

"I make the motion that we vote Olaf in as our first sheriff, and he must have the cooperation of every man here. We must establish a town council and give them the authority to do what needs to be done. May I see a show of hands?"

Every hand went up.

A hoarse voice called, "I'm parched. Where's the refreshments?"

I had wondered at Olaf's well-spoken words, at his presence as he stood in front of that noisy group. He had the skill of a seasoned orator. Most of the townspeople, both French and Norwegian, still spoke with the unmistakable dialect of the old country.

Later Bessie told me that Helga had lodged the boys in Thief River Falls for the winter months when they were ready for high school. Few students in Obeege claimed that advantage, but it came at a price. Helga had suffered the long, cold winter caring for her other children and the livestock, doing whatever was necessary to keep the farm alive. Now, listening to Olaf, I knew Helga's sacrifice had not been in vain.

When I closed the door, it was after four AM, and I was exhilarated by the night's results—at least, I thought it was exhilaration as I wobbled home through the snow, guided by the dim beam of a flashlight.

The house was dark and something seemed wrong with these damn matches. I had struck half a dozen before I got the lamp lit. The wall hanger seemed to resist my every effort to accept the heavy coat so when it fell to the floor, I kicked it aside and thought, serves it right, lay there all night for all I care.

The sounds of my clumsy attempts to make coffee woke Bessie and she stormed into the kitchen.

"Fritz, are you drunk?"

Carefully forming every syllable, I mumbled, "Of course I'm not drunk. What a ridiculous question. What's wrong with this coffeepot?"

"Where have you been until nearly five o'clock?"

"Making history, my dear." With that, I gave her a big sloppy kiss that she wasn't quick enough to dodge. Then I told her of the plans we had put in motion and, as I enthused, she made the coffeepot work.

I got a little steadier on my feet, and when she said, "Let's go to bed," I didn't need to be coaxed. I was exhausted and all I wanted was sleep.

With bleary eyes, I followed her into the bedroom as she carried the lamp. By the soft light I could see her hair was down and lay shining against the pink of her nightgown. I leaned and kissed that smooth skin somewhere below her ear.

I stumbled on the rug. My eyes couldn't seem to see anything but the rhythmic movement of that lovely round place where her hips joined and the breasts, without restraint, fascinated me. She smelled so good.

She put the lamp down, and I quickly blew it out and reached for her. She held me at arm's length without difficulty, but after a few moments of struggle, Bessie said, "Fritz! Fritz, put me down!" as I teetered unsteadily.

"This is entirely inappropriate for folks our age. For goodness sake, we're seventy years old. Stop this foolishness— you know what Mrs. Melby said."

Then she giggled like a high-school girl and asked "Woof-woof?"

But after all that, I put her back on her feet. My spirit was willing, but I could feel my flesh getting weak. I tumbled into bed cuddled against her. Apparently Mrs. Melby hadn't mentioned the evils of cuddling or the possibilities, I thought, but then I heard her soft snore. I went to sleep.

CHAPTER 12

I slept late so I hurried down to the bar. As usual, Helmer met me at the door, hammer in hand. I knew when that hammer connected with the nail, my head would burst.

"Let's have some coffee and talk," I said, hoping to distract him. My hands shook and my stomach with no good intentions lay in wait for that coffee.

"Hey, Perfesser, it's almost noon. Yer late. See? I brung my hammer. I'm gonna nail that hinge on, but that can wait. Thought I'd help you clean up too. Guess the fellas really celebrated the election. 'Bout four o'clock, wasn't it? And we had a new sheriff. We sure got the job done," Helmer crowed. "Olaf wuz smilin' ear to ear and Fritz, you wuz the big push."

"No, I wasn't. It was a group effort. It was your idea, and those ladies were certainly up in arms and with us all the way. That's a force to seriously consider. Bessie would have revoked my house privileges if…"

"Talk English, Perfesser," said Helmer in an aggravated voice. "I've only got six grades behind me an' lucky to have

that. You kin tell yer wife for me, she pushed a damn good job tha
shoulda got done a long time ago. Olaf sure looks good behind
that badge, don't he? 'Course it's Orren the ladies always cozy up
to. He's got a line of bullshit that hooks 'em every time, but you'll
notice it's always Olaf that reels 'em in. Still water runs deep, ya
know. Hey, this cup got a hole in the bottom."

I made no response. Just reached for the pot, filled his cup, and
pushed the last of the sugar cubes his way.

"Hi, honey. Sure is good to come home. I'm tired—had a long
day. If you haven't started supper yet, turn on the radio—let's see
if we can get Amos and Andy. Nope, nothing but static. Guess
spring is official. See the kids are out of school. The town sure
looks different now that Olaf has got people cleaning up the trash
around. You can actually walk on the street after only three weeks.
The man is a dynamo. Helga must be so proud of him. We should
have done this years ago."

"Fritz, when are those WPA guys going to finish that ditch? It's
a muddy eyesore."

"Yes, but the downtown merchants will be glad for the water
main. Should be done next month, I hear. Olaf has done a good
job. The dances and other activities have become downright
civilized. He's organized these town meetings and both the Nordic
and the French are exchanging ideas instead of fisticuffs and, for
the first time, they can say hello when they pass in the street. He
deputized Orren and another fellow and added two Frenchies.
They're working together without a hitch. Olaf doesn't put up with
any foolishness, so he's got the town's attention and respect. We did
ourselves a favor when we put him in charge."

"Fritz, I really want to go to the dance. Fourth of July comes only once a year, so don't be such a stick-in-the mud. I hear on the party line that there's a new man in the band with a violin. Everybody will be there. I'd like a chance to talk to Mrs. Melby—I hear the store is doing big business now that Marguerite is there. Seems like all the local fellows have developed a taste for soup even in this hot weather. Mrs. Melby says Orren is spending time with the pastor's daughter."

"What do you women do all day besides gossip on the party line?"

"Oh, let me see. Okay, cooking, cleaning, weeding the garden, washing, keeping the woodbox filled, milking the cows when the head of the house is still down at Sorenson's playing pool, fixing a ten o'clock supper when he gets home late, taking care of the kids…"

"Bessie, Bessie!"

"Oh, yes, don't let us forget her marital duties after the fun stuff is done."

"All right, all right. Damn sorry I asked. Let me help you with that lamp. Either you'll have oil all over you or you'll break the chimney again. Now I'll have to smell burnt hair."

"Fritz, this isn't going to be a happy evening if I apply this curling iron to you, believe me, it won't be smelling like burnt hair where I am going to put it."

"Bessie!"

"Honey, don't be upset. Let's walk over to the hall, the evening has cooled down. I want to see all the flags up and visit a little with folks. C'mon, it won't take fifteen minutes."

"Bessie, I've only been on my feet for ten hours at that noisy bar, but anything to please you. It's been busy all day and some of the bunch were getting pretty ugly. That's why I'm home early. I'm a little worried. I hope Olaf and his deputies can keep things quiet. If there is any rough stuff, we'll come home, okay? Are you going to wear that blue dress? You look good in that even if it is a little short."

"Don't worry about the length of my dress. When you were young, you would have noticed sooner that I have the legs for it."

"Well, I may feel younger when we get home tonight, so we'll talk more about your legs when I blow out the light. What's taking you so long? Hurry it up, my feet are killing me."

We hurried and my feet endured.

"See, it only took us fifteen minutes. I think everyone in the county is in town. Oh, listen to that fiddle—that's an improvement. Oh, there's Helga with Buddy and Frankie. Ila's holding the baby. Marguerite came along, I hear. Doesn't Ila look pretty? Her hair has grown. This is the first time she's been to a dance since Charbeneau. Dance me over there so we can talk."

"Hush up and dance. You've always got the party line, so hush. This is our favorite waltz, remember? Remember the pavilion at Maple Lake? We didn't miss a dance. You had your hair all bobbed and silk stockings with a seam in the back that wouldn't stay straight. Oh, yes, I noticed your legs. I fell in love with you that night."

"But you were too bashful to even kiss me goodnight. Fritz! You're squeezing the breath out of me. Don't you dare muss up my hair."

I felt a tap on my shoulder that interrupted this tender moment and turned my head to see Bjournson's grinning face.

"Hey, Fritz! This is Tag Waltz," he said as he danced Bessie away until I lost sight of her in the whirl of the enthusiastic dancers. I cussed to myself and wandered off to shoot the bull with the fellows.

"Fritz, you've been gone for hours. Where have you been? Helga and the kids went home hours ago."

"I've been checking the crowd. The moonshine is flowing like a river. It is so noisy and smoky, I'm nearly blind. Can't get near the dance floor. Look at Lars—he's passed out on the keyboard and the fiddler's gone. Who could dance just to a harmonica but this bunch."

"I'm ready. Take my hand. All this pushing and shoving…"

"See that man over there in the green shirt? That's Morrissey. He's been trying to start trouble all night. Olaf is trying to keep the peace, but it's building up to a real brawl, I'm afraid. Hurry. Oh, hell—there it blows! Olaf right in the middle of it. Where in hell is Orren? Oh, there he is with a couple of fellows. Looks like a free-for-all. Will you stop screaming? Head for the door."

"Hi, Helmer. Well, if it isn't the town crier. Haven't seen you for a while. Helga must be keeping you busy. The coffee's about ready. Will you join me in a cup?"

"You don't hafta ask. Glad this fourth is over. Saw you and your missus at the dance, but you skipt out too soon and missed the good part."

"We must not have been at the same dance. I didn't see any good part."

"Yeah, fer sure, it did get rough."

"What was Morrissey so damned crazy about?"

"Well, Fritz, they wuz both courtin' the same woman and she married Lazorre. Morrissey never got over it and that wuz three years ago. He's been trackin' Lazorre lookin' fer trouble ever since. Found it that night when he pushed Lazorre's wife and she fell. Lazorre swing on him and the fight wuz on. You know them French men love to fight, specially when they're all likkered up, and they wuz about drownin' in moonshine that night. 'Bout thirty of 'em mixin' it up. Olaf and his deputies right in the middle of it. People tryin' to get out, crowdin' the door, wimmin screamin', kids cryin'." He stopped for breath.

"Yeah, I can see I missed the good part."

Before he continued his story, he pushed his cup out for a refill.

"Took Olaf four deputies to finally break it up and get Morrissey to the Fosston lockup. He's a mean bastard and quick on his feet—got Olaf in a bad place. Slowed him down a little. Now that the damn ditch is finished, do you think the WPA will build us our own jail?"

"I doubt it."

"Olaf said he'd keep Morrissey in jail for a while till he cooled off. Morrissey swears he'll kill both Lazorre and Olaf. Just talk I spose, but they better watch themselves.

"I went on home and heard Orren drive in late. Guess he musta been with Olaf helpin' out at the jail. Haven't seen Olaf with a woman since he got home from that fishin' trip. Must be he's planning on bein' a bachelor. He's awful edgy lately—workin' too hard.

"Well, I better git on home. Orren and me are puttin' up hay and next week I'll be shucking corn. See you later, Fritz."

CHAPTER 13

"Howdy, Fritz. Just stopped by for a minute. I've been tryin' to catch up with Olaf—he got away early this morning. Last night he drove in with a big box. I figgered it wuz sumpthin for the jail. You know he's been fixin' that up and it's lookin' better than a jail should. Well, he brung this box in and set it down and that baby girl ran to him and lifted her arms. She laughed and said 'Daddee' just as plain. He blushed, can you believe our tough sheriff blushed? Red as a beet and hid his face in her curls.

"Helga laughed, poked him in the ribs and said, 'Son, does that baby know something I don't?' Marguerite jist turned her head. Them wimmin!

"Well, we crowded around and watched him open that box and pull out a pink and white high chair. He scooped that baby up and put her in it and you can't believe the look on his face."

"How's he feeling?" I asked. "Is he still walkin' funny?"

"No, he sure is a good-lookin' man. He'll make some lucky

girl a fine husband. That shiner Morrissey hung on him is about gone too. Must be over a week since he got outta jail. Olaf told him to stay out of town. Morrissey said he wuz goin' back to Canady. Good riddance.

"Gotta go, Fritz. Got about two more days puttin' up hay, then we're on to the cornfield. I'm sure not lookin' forward to that. Forty acres of corn—about twenty acres too many, I'd say, specially since I'm coverin' for Orren. He's still spendin' a lot of time with the pastor's daughter—he's got it bad with this one. Them stalks are seven feet high and so thick and heavy with cobs. Rows are almost a quarter of a mile long and dark. The sun can hardly get through. We'll be shuckin' corn and shovelin' through the snow to the corn crib till Santa comes down the chimney. Gotta go—see you later."

A couple of days later, yawning and scratching, I made it to the kitchen and kissed the back of Bessie's neck.

"Morning, Bessie. Hey, you're looking good, but you looked better last night and the lights weren't even on."

"Yes, and when it's daylight all you want to do is eat. Will you stop that!"

"Well, all that exercise makes me hungry. How about a cup of coffee for starters? And make those eggs sunny-side up. Damn that phone—let it ring. Is the toast in? Let it ring."

"But Fritz, that's Helga's ring—two long and a short," she protested, but I hung tough.

"Will you please pour the coffee?"

"Can't you wait until it's perked? Wonder why anybody is calling Helga this early."

"That's all right, Bessie," I said with all the sarcasm I could muster before breakfast. "I can find my way to the coffeepot. I realize how important it is for you to start the day right. Don't worry about my breakfast—I'm just your husband. Would you dump this burned toast when you find time?"

I thought that would surely get some attention.

"Damn, I hate the smell of burnt eggs. What? What? What about Olaf? Lucky devil, he's had his breakfast and he'll be in Fosston by now."

Bessie turned from the phone with a look of horror on her face. "Fritz, Fritz! Something terrible has happened. Lazorre is dead—murdered."

"What? What? Give me the phone."

I snatched it from her and pushed her back.

"Fritz, what's he saying? What?"

"Morrissey, that son of a bitch, printed in blood on the barn door, 'One down. One to go.' Olaf is organizing a search party, and I'm going down to help. He said for Helga to pick up Marguerite. Everything in town in locked down and you do the same. Don't open the door to anybody. I'll be home as soon as I can."

"Bessie, I've been trying to get through on this damn phone for hours. Will you women get off that party line?"

"We're just trying to find out what happened."

"Well, here it is. A neighbor went to Lazorre's to return some tool that he'd borrowed. He said he heard the cows in the barn making such a racket that he went directly there. Found the dog dead and a sign on the door, 'One down. One to go,' printed in blood. Barely dry. In the barn was Lazorre with the pitchfork in his back and his throat cut—blood everywhere. That Morrissey is damned quick with a knife."

I heard Bessie's quick intake of breath.

"Olaf figured Lazorre had been milking with his back turned, sitting on a stool. He never had a chance. The neighbor turned the cows out—they were crazed by the smell. He went to the house and found the wife on the floor unconscious and beaten so badly he hardly recognized her. He called Olaf then. He said the kids had spent the night with Gramma—there had been a birthday party. Only last night it had been a happy family and now it's almost destroyed. I'll be home in a couple of hours. Don't bother with cooking—I couldn't eat a thing. Keep the house locked."

CHAPTER 14

"Helmer! Where have you been keeping yourself? Seems like a month since you've been in. How about a cup of coffee— it still is coffee, isn't it?"

"Yeah, I decided to give God another chance."

My eyebrows raised at Helmer's magnanimous decision.

I poured the coffee and pushed the bowl of sugar cubes over to him, then settled myself on a nearby stool.

"I heard you were cooking for yourself again and I'm sorry to hear that. Thought you had it made at Torgerson's."

I really did feel sorry for Helmer. He looked like whipped pup.

"Well, everything went downhill when Olaf got shot. I'm leavin' for North Dakota as soon as the fall's work is done and he gets on his feet. The neighbors got all the hay in, but the corn is rottin' in that jungle."

I couldn't contain my curiosity. "Helmer, what in hell happened in that cornfield?"

"It's a long story with a piss-poor ending. Thanks for the

coffee, Fritz. Gotta go now. I know you're wantin' to get the place cleaned up."

"It's still early—I've got time. Come on, Helmer, let's hear it. Come on."

He picked up his spoon, and stirred his coffee. The look on his face darkened, and suddenly he looked old and tired.

"I don't know where to start."

"At the beginning, Helmer."

"Well, that woulda been 'bout thirty years ago, and I think this must be the end of it."

I refilled his cup and he added another sugar cube while I fidgeted.

He spoke so slowly and quietly that I had to lean forward to hear.

"When I came in for supper that night, I saw the kids' stick horses that Olaf had made and painted. One wuz black and white—that wuz Spot. The other wuz Buster. The reins of the braided twine bridle were pushed through the latticework of the porch. The boys were kickin' each other under the table laughin' and talkin'. 'Hey, Ma, did you know there is Indians in the cornfield? We seen one.' 'Did not! Wuzn't no feathers and tomihawks.' 'Did so—ow! Ma...' You know how boys are, Fritz. Their ma said, 'Will you sit up straight and stop that kicking right now. Eat your supper and hush. Stay out of that cornfield—you'll get lost. Do I have to smack you?'

"The boys ate fast and headed for the door as Helga hollered, 'Now remember what I told you—stay close. It will soon be dark.' I wuz just finishing when Olaf drove in. Helga wuz tidyin' up, but Marguerite wuz fixin' him a big plate when he opened the door. He wuz carryin' a 30-30 rifle—the one he used for deer—and he handed it to me. Ast me to load it for him while he ate. 'Hang it on the gun rack in the pickup, Helmer,' he told me, 'and don't bother with the safety. I'll check it when I get to town. Where's Orren?'

"Helga turned and answered, 'He ate earlier. Said he had business in town.'

" 'Yeah? He's probably over at the pastor's house making sure that blonde daughter is safe, or maybe he's getting saved. He'd better be taking care of business.'

"I barely heard Helga say, 'So much for his "ruined" life,' and heard Marguerite giggle.

" 'What's that, Ma?'

" 'Nothing, any news of Morrissey?'

" 'No, about twenty of us were pushing through the woods. Some of that is mighty rough country. Well, we did find the Hupmobile he stold from Lazorre. Had two flat tires and an empty gas tank. It wuz all covered with brush. Guess he planned to drive to the border—it's only about ninety miles. But there's no trace of him. Seems like he just vanished into thin air. It's been almost two weeks and we figger he's long gone. The Royal Canadian Mounties will be waiting for him. We figger he'll try to sneak across. If he makes it, the mounties will catch him some day and he'll hang. Everybody has been shut down pretty tight, of course, but now folks are starting to relax and that sure is a good feeling.'

" 'More coffee, son?'

" 'No, Ma, gotta go. Well, maybe haffa cup.'

"I went on out with the gun, loaded it and put it in the pickup, then walked down to the barn to milk. Olaf came out a little later and Helga called after him, 'Will you yell for those dratted boys? I told them to stay close, so where could they have gone? I told them to stay out of that cornfield.'

"Then Olaf wuz yelling for the kids, but there wuz no answer. I put the milk pail down and walked with him to the cornfield behind the barn. The sun had just started to set. I felt a shiver, but shrugged it off. Olaf wuz yellin', 'Buddy, Frankie' over and over, and then we heard 'em cryin'.

" 'Thank God,' Olaf said. 'I hope Ma blisters their asses. Finish your milking, Helmer. I'll bring them out.' He walked down between the rows. I couldn't bring myself to leave or put away the sight of him as the tall stalks closed behind.

"Sumpthin nagged at me. Sumpthin, but what? What the hell—it's only a cornfield. I shrugged it off.

"I could hear his voice growin' fainter and the kids answerin', and I thought for sure by now he must… The I heard the shot, then, louder still, the sudden silence and I knew—I knew! The boys had been the bait and this time Olaf wuz at the wrong end of the pole. The sickenin' truth took root—truth that we had paid no mind to the boys' playful talk of the 'Indian.' We had allowed ourselves to know what we wanted to believe, that Morrissey wuz in Canada.

"I ran to the truck and pulled the gun from the rack. It seemed weightless as I pushed my way through the cornfield followin' the path that Olaf had taken, runnin' to save the life of the man who wuz my son."

"Helmer! Your son?"

"Yes, yes, my son! My own flesh and blood."

I was astounded! Who would ever have guessed? But I knew this wasn't the time.

"In the last rays of the sun, I saw Morrissey as he stood,

his arm upraised, flung back. Without lifting the gun to my shoulder, I pointed it, pulled the trigger, and sent him straight to hell.

"Fritz, please, just a short one? Please?"

"Hell, no, you're talking to the wrong man. Get on with it."

"I dropped the gun and fell on my knees beside Olaf. The burnt hole in the front of his shirt marked the blood trail the bullet had taken on its way to his heart. 'Olaf, Olaf,' I begged, but there wuz no sound other than that of the screamin' kids. Then there wuz a boy on each side of me, holdin' tight to my hand as we ran between the rows, stumblin', fallin', strugglin' to our feet, only to do it all over again, chokin' for breath.

"I heard Helga's voice from somewhere and I figgered she'd heard the shots when she came to the barn to help me milk. We connected part way and she followed the path toward the heavy smell of gun powder where her son lay.

"Fritz, just one, in the name of God!"

"Don't even ask. I said no! Are you deaf? No. No! Finish your story."

"Marguerite wuz waitin' at the barn with a lantern. The kids jist fell into her and when she could talk, she said that Orren wuz on his way. She gave me the lantern and I found the old army cot I had given the boys for their fort. Thinking that cot would serve as a stretcher, I grabbed it and a blanket from my bunk and hurried back to those I'd never claimed.

"The silence wuz broken only by the soft rustle of the nightbirds' wings as they flew to escape the sound of my ragged breathin' and Helga's frantic prayers.

"I sunk down on the dirt beside her and reached for Olaf's

hand, my hand slippery with his blood, and found such a faint, irregular throb of life that all hope left me.

"By the flickerin' light of the lantern, Helga wuz tryin' to stop the flow of blood with her apron. As I wiped the blood from his face, my fingers traced the hideous yawn that carved his temple to the jawbone, and I knew what Morrissey had held in his upraised hand. I pulled the blanket higher so Helga wouldn't see.

"The black blood pooled beneath us as we clung together. It seemed like an eternity till the lights of the lanterns blurred like fireflies in the far distance. Then the blessed sound of voices came near.

"The doctor at Thief River Falls wuz quick. 'There is no exit wound. I believe the bullet plowed through his upper lung and lodged very near his heart. We have neither the equipment nor the expertise—you'll only find that at St. Luke's Hospital in St. Paul. It's a three-hour drive in the ambulance. We'll give him a blood transfusion and our prayers that he will arrive there alive. It is his only chance.'

"Helga followed the gurney. When she came back she wuz buttonin' her sleeve. She turned to Orren. 'Bring us clean clothes and we'll meet up in St Paul. Hurry.'

"I took her hand and we ran to the ambulance.

"The steady hum of the big motor as we raced with time along the dark road wuz broken only by my feeble attempts of comfort as I lied to both of us. 'He's young and strong—I know he's goin' to make it." Helga wuz chokin', 'My son, my son.' She held my hand so tight it wuz numb when the ambulance stopped at the big brick buildin' that wuz St. Luke's.

"The doctors were waitin' and Olaf wuz wheeled away.

We were shown to a small room where we waited in the quiet as the door closed the busy sounds away.

"In the bright lights, our bloody clothes kept the horrible scene alive. I wuz relieved when Orren hurried in carryin' a suitcase that soon bulged with our cast-offs.

"I mumbled to Orren, 'On my way home, I'll dump them.' But Helga heard me and reached out, sayin' 'No, you stay.'

"Then came the bone-chillin' verdict from the doctor.

" 'The bullet is lodged just a few inches from his heart. The lung has been torn badly, causing a tremendous loss of blood. We recommend a long and dangerous operation—it is his only chance. Your decision, Madam.'

"Helga didn't hesitate. She said, "Do it—we are your donors.'

"The night dragged on like a lifetime in the silence of that antiseptic little room interrupted only by Orren's hoarse breathing and Helga's comforting words.

"My thoughts of Morrissey's destroyed head stirred the deeply buried memories of the war that I'd hidden all these years in the depth of my gut. True, I'd carried a gun there, but it hadn't been so up close and personal. I couldn't seem to get warm or stop shakin'.

"Long, agonizin' hours later, the door opened and the tired voice of the surgeon told us that they recovered the bullet and Olaf had made it through the surgery. The next three days will be crucial, he said, adding that they closed the 'ugly gash on his face,' but that he would always carry a scar.

" 'Why don't you folks go down to the cafeteria and have something to eat,' the doctor suggested. 'The coffee is very good too.'

"Late in the afternoon on the third day, the doctor seemed triumphant when he briefed us. 'His vital signs are better than we expected. Of course, he hasn't regained consciousness, but we believe the worst is over.'

"As his mother collapsed, Orren caught her and laid her on a bed. My knees turned to water and I stumbled back into the chair where I had lain awake on those nights, dreadin' what morning might bring. Orren had tried to sleep in the truck and now he said, 'I've got to get out of here for a while.' I heard the door swing shut.

"I closed my eyes and all the dead men I'd ever seen were waitin' there, standin' at attention. They all had Morrissey's shattered face. My eyes jerked open and I heard myself scream.

"Helga stood there, her hand outstretched. Her eyes blurred with the tears that always seemed to be brimmin'.

"On my feet now, I reached for her. She stepped toward me and put her arms 'round my waist, her head on my chest. My arms wrapped 'round her and drew her into my very being, where she had lived every minute for over thirty years. I thought my heart would burst with the overflowin' love that consumed me, and I knew my life had meanin' only in the circle of her arms.

" 'I was sixteen,' she said, 'the first time you held me like this. And then you were gone. I knew before Olaf was born that I should have waited for you, but I was young and scared and pregnant....'

"Before God, Fritz, I never knew till I got home and she wuz married. And now my fears and common sense came floodin' in, knowin' that this turrible experience with Olaf had blinded her. I thought she would hate me when she realized that.

"What did I have to give her? I'd been a drunk for years and now I wuz only her reformed hired hand, livin' in the bunkhouse. All I owned to my name wuz a shack on an overgrown piece of land and a change of clothes, but how could I let her go?

"I wuz numb when I kissed her tears away and smoothed her hair back with my tremblin' fingers.

"Fritz, I can't..., I can't..."

"Yes, you can. Finish it."

"As I looked down, she lifted her arms and pulled my head to hers and kissed me fully on the mouth. The door opened and Orren walked in, hesitated, then grinned and said, 'Well, Unk, or has the title changed?'

"As the torment raged in my soul, I pushed her arms away, put her hand in Orren's, and left the room. I walked to find the nearest bar to drown myself in total oblivion. Surely God would understand. He wuz a lovin' God, wuzn't He? He had to know I wuz a weak man, that I could never live up to Helga's expectations.

"I lay unconscious on a wooden bench somewhere that night. When I waked up, Morrissey wore his own face in hell, and I knew I had joined him there.

"Later I walked past the bar and all my senses begged for the 'hair of the dog,' but my feet were deaf to all their pleadin'. I made it to the cafeteria where I had several cups of black coffee that stayed with me till I made it to the men's room with a head that threatened to explode. I forced myself to go back to the little room where I knew Helga waited.

"She looked at me as I stood in the doorway. 'You've been drinking.' In her eyes I read the prayer that I could deny it.

" 'Yes,' I answered.

" 'Then you're not the man I thought you were.'

"And I knew she wuz right.

"Her words burned through my raw consciousness, along with that unbearable, unforgivin' knowledge that once again I'd failed and lost forever her love that had been given so freely. Now where wuz God when I needed Him? Hell, hadn't I given it a good try? Almost four months on the wagon workin' hard, lookin' good. Hadn't I honored my promise to Him? Why had He allowed that bar to be right in my path? Right there, right then? I raged against Him as I stomped down the sidewalk. It wuz His fault. He could have given me the strength to walk past. He promised never to forsake me. Empty promises. It's not my fault, it's His.

"I wuz so cursin' mad at God for His failins that I didn't see the curb. Off balance, I fell and the gutter claimed one of its own.

"Strugglin' to my feet, cussin' to myself, but being careful not to use God's name in vain lest He raise up another curb to trip me, I finally found the truck in the parking lot, with the keys hidden where Orren always left them—under the seat cover on the passenger side.

"The cool morning air suddenly seemed stiflin'. I rolled the window down, lay my head back, and closed my eyes. I could smell the fragrant winter hay that Orren and I had just brung in. It wuz stacked twelve feet high in the old barn. I knew where the ropes were hung, coiled on the hanger, out of the way. Didn't have to be a fancy knot, the jump would break my neck and I'd have peace at last. I'd be done with this empty senseless life.

"The decision wuz so warm, so comfortin' that I could hardly wait. My hand wuz steady as I leaned forward with the key.

"Suddenly Orren's strained face appeared at the window. Frantic, he said, 'You get sober, Unk. I can't do this alone. I'm scared—what if Olaf doesn't make it? What if he has a relapse? I need your help. Help me, Unk, for Ma's sake if you truly love her. Help us now. I can't handle everything by myself. We are your family—you can't leave us. Promise me, Unk, promise!'

"It wuz with a curious sense of relief that I heard myself say, 'I promise. Together we can do it all. I promise you.' And I knew the ship had sailed and I wuz still on the dock.

"Well, Fritz, there it is. You're lookin' like you got a gut full of Bjournson's best corn likker—before it wuz done cookin'. This may be goodbye. As soon as Olaf is on his feet, I'm headin' for North Dakota."

"You didn't ask for my opinion, Helmer, but I'm going to give it to you anyway. I think you ought to give those medals back, the ones you got for bravery, the ones your father was so proud of. Give them back. They pinned them on the wrong person. You're a damned coward, and I'm ashamed of you. They should have given them to Helga. She had the guts, the courage to come to you, and you didn't have the backbone to meet her like a man. You ran off and hid behind the bottle. What has she hidden behind, all these years? You coward. I'm ashamed of you. Here, take this bottle with you. No charge."

"You can go to hell, Fritz, and keep your damn whiskey—it's probably watered down anyway."

CHAPTER 15

The tantalizing smell of bacon, the sizzle of the eggs frying, the faint odor of burned toast on the back of the stove permeated the kitchen where the two boys sat.

"We wuz way down in that cornfield, Ma. We didn't see that Indian, right off. He just seemed to be there. He scart us real bad. Frankie cried."

"Did not!"

"Did too!"

"Well, you cried too."

"Not until he told us to shut the hell up and pushed me so hard I fell down. Then I got real scart, and we wuz so glad to hear Olaf yellin' for us. The Indian laughed and said, 'Come 'n get it, pretty boy.' I wondered what wuz funny. Then we heard the gun go bang and Olaf fell down and the Indian wuz holding him by the hair and we seen the knife too.

"Ma, are you cryin'? We won't ever run away again, Ma. Don't cry, don't cry."

"Finish your breakfast, boys, and go tend to your horses. I think I hear Spot."

"Yeah, c'mon, Frankie."

Olaf stepped into the kitchen and sat down at the big table.

"Ma, is the coffeepot still on? I'm tired of doing nothing. The doc said to take it easy for a month, and I've done that. It's time for me to get up and give Orren some help. He must be tired doing my job and keeping up with the work here. Thank God for Unk. Where is he anyhow? Has he grown fast to that bunkhouse?"

"I haven't seen him lately. We had a difference of opinion, and he doesn't come to the house very often, and then only to ask about you. Don't worry about Orren—he can't be too tired. It's every night at the pastor's house, but he's home early. The pastor has declared a curfew, and Oren is chafing at the bit. He's actually talking about marriage for the first time. The pastor said if they'd wait a year, he'd finance a house."

"Well, that's decent of him. How old is she??

"Only seventeen, but she will be eighteen in two weeks. Guess there had been a party planned, but it's been canceled. Daddy's decision. He called me yesterday and was sure hot under the collar. 'Mrs. Torgerson,' he said, 'I have had to seriously reprimand your son and have told him to make other plans for at least a month. Needless to say, he has been very uncooperative, and I'd like you to reinforce my decision.' "

"Well, Ma, you know his reputation. Love 'em and leave 'em. I can't say I blame the pastor. I wonder what he caught Orren up to?"

"It seems she has some large red splotches on her neck and shoulders. Don't laugh, Olaf—Orren was raised better than that. What's so funny?"

"I've noticed Orren with more than a few of those red splotches under his collar too. First time I ever knew hickies were contagious."

"Don't worry, Ma, I'll talk to him. Where has Marguerite hidden my clothes? That woman is killing me with kindness."

"You must be blind, Olaf, that woman is in love with you."

"Well, she'd be an easy woman to love, for sure, but just look at me. This ugly face—will it ever heal? I look like hell. I'm sure not the man I was. She can do better."

"Son, that scar will fade. Give it some time, have patience. And don't underestimate Marguerite. She loves you and not for your face."

"You're putting words in her mouth, Ma. Don't be matchmaking."

"Just a little unasked-for advice. You'd better give this some serious thought. I worry that you're going to miss the best thing that could happen to you. I can see the way you act around her, the way your eyes follow her. You aren't a lovesick schoolboy, you are a man. A man in love, and it shows. Tell her you love her, for goodness sake, let her make her own decision."

"Ma! Will you stop?"

"Not yet. She's young and beautiful with a lifetime ahead of her, and with two children to consider. She will put their welfare, their security first, and some lucky man will be giving Baby Doll piggyback rides and teaching Frankie how to ride a horse."

"Damn it to hell, Ma! If you must have the truth—I don't dare to love her. I'm scared and I don't scare easy. What if she rejects me? I don't know if I'm man enough to stand up to that."

"I don't believe it's fear. It's your stiff-necked manly pride. You came by it honestly, you and your pride! You are so like your father. Why don't you take your manly pride and join him in his shack. You can both feel manly and sorry for yourselves and each other."

"Ma, what are you telling me? I don't understand."

"Talk to Helmer. It's time you knew the truth."

"Ma, what in hell are you saying?"

My fingers tightened on the bar towel as I looked up to see Helmer standing in the doorway, the door closing quietly.

"Fritz, do I dare come in?"

"I don't know what to say, Helmer. I didn't expect to see you again after our last conversation."

"Well, for a man who doesn't know what to say, I'd guess you'd think of sumpthin. But ferget it. That talkin'-to wuz sumpthin I needed to hear, and I appreciate you givin' it to me straight. Any coffee in that pot? I've been drinkin' a lot of that this last month, stayin' home and tryin' to get my head on right. I've decided to give it another try, and I know I'll get it right this time."

Helmer looked thoughtfully into his cup as though he was counting the sugar cubes.

"I wanta to tell you, Fritz. Sumpthin happened to me up there in that dark, miserable shack. One night—or I thought it wuz night, but it coulda been mornin' 'cause it wuz so light.

My ma wuz sittin' there in her apron. She wuz smilin' when she leaned over and kissed me. She said real quiet like, 'My son, my son, God has not given up on you, and you must know that I never will. He will give you the strength to be the man you were meant to be, but you must—must—help yourself.' I felt her hands as they pulled my blanket higher.

"Fritz, it's time I help myself—it's time."

He paused for a moment, his voice breaking, then said, "With God and two good women in my corner, how can I fail?"

"Count me in, Helmer. I'll join the group. I'm with you all the way." I struggled to keep my own voice steady.

"Oh, almost forgot! Olaf was in last night looking for you. He looked a little upset, so I hope everything is okay."

"Yeah, always sumpthin, you know. See you later."

He opened the door and I heard the honk of a car, then Olaf's voice.

"Hey, Unk, wait up. I've been looking for you. I'm driving over to Fosston to check things at the jail. Wanta ride along?"

"Sure. Glad to see you up and around. You've had a close call."

"Yeah, and Ma about finished me off this morning and took care of you at the same time. She told me that I was stiff-necked, prideful, and blind, just like you. Actually, she said, 'just like your father.' How do you plead?"

"Slow down, Olaf. Slow down, you're gonna put us in the ditch. Guess the CCC boys haven't worked this road yet."

"Unk? Father? Dad? Get to it, Helmer. Are you my father?"

"Yes, I am your father. We are of the same blood, but you are Ole's son. He raised you to be the man you are. I won't take that away from him. He gave the family a good life and died too young."

"What about you and Ma?"

You sure you wanta hear this?"

"I'm real sure."

"It wuz wartime and we wuz young and later we got scart. I came home for my ma's funeral a couple of months before Ole got out on a medical. Then I got shipped out. I never knew Helga wuz pregnant. When I got home, one look and I knew you were mine and probably Ole did too, but we both loved her and we let it go. It is enough for me that you know now. Call me 'Unk,' we don't want gossip."

"Well, Unk, guess it's guilty as charged. I wonder if I haven't always known this deep down. There's always been a special place for you as long as I can remember. I loved my dad, but there was always you. I want you to know that I would have died there in that cornfield, but I felt you there with me. And in the hospital on that cold, white table, I knew somehow in some unexplainable way, you were there. No one but God and you and me."

CHAPTER 16

"Hey, Fritz, yer open on time today—what's happenin'?"

"Morning, Helmer. Yeah, I'm out early trying to get this mess cleaned up. Some of the boys were in last night celebrating somebody's birthday. Didn't clear out till damn near one o'clock. Teaching school was a helluva lot easier. I need a break—let's have a cup of coffee. What's happening with you?"

"Well, Fritz, I need some advice. Bjournson came by a coupla days ago. Guess he's heard I'm gonna try North Dakota for a while. He offered me seven hundred dollars for the forty acres, but I figger if he waters down his moonshine, he's done the same with his offer and I'm gonna come out on the short end. Hell, Fritz, I don't know nuthin' about real estate. Of course, he brung along a jug to prime me, but I told him I had sworn off, that I wuz a different man. He laughed at me and said, 'Again? I'll save it for you.' Well, he'll be too old to sugar his mash or remember where he hid the vat before he pours one for me. Even the smell made me sick to my stomach."

"Helmer, in case you haven't noticed, we are in the middle of a hellish depression. Men are standing in breadlines in the big cities or begging for a job for a dollar a day. The economy went to hell after the war. Why would you want to sell now? Land is at rock-bottom prices. I've had my house and this bar for sale all summer and not a bite. I wouldn't do it, but I promised Bessie."

Helmer scratched his head, but he didn't sound convinced.

"If I had a little startup money, I could try my luck in North Dakota. I've got an old army buddy there who'd be glad to see me. You know I ain't got nuthin' goin' for me here, Fritz."

"Hell's fire, you could have! You're young—early fifties? You're going to stay sober and get a new start, so why not here? What about Helga? You going to run away from her too?"

"Wish I could give you a different answer, Fritz, but after that last drunk, I don't stand a chance and you know it."

"I don't know it. Women are strange creatures. They always seem to do the opposite of what you expect. You talk about giving yourself another chance, well, why don't you get big-hearted and give Helga another chance?" I pulled out all the stops.

"Helga needs you as much as you need her. I'm not the only one who's noticed you and Olaf have more in common than those funny-colored eyes. To say nothing of the way you both toe out on the left foot. Well, to get back to the land deal—I say sell it if you can get your price, and the going price is less than two dollars an acre. Sell it, but stay right here. This town is on the move. There will be better opportunities here than on that godforsaken North Dakota prairie.

"Yesterday I heard Mrs. Lazorre sold her property to a lumber company, so she's back on her feet. Guess she's going home to her folks. The company wants to establish a sawmill right here on the river. Mrs. Melby said she rented the two upstairs rooms to a young doctor who wants to start his own practice. And Olaf is trying to raise money to add a room to the schoolhouse. This town has a future and so do you," I told him, laying a hand on his shoulder.

"Maybe, if I had someone to share it with."

"You better give it some serious thought. Aren't you tired of running?"

Changing the subject, I asked, "What does that big-time moonshiner want with your land?"

"It's the water. He's desperate for water. He's got two big stills hid out there in the brush cookin' up a hundred and thirty gallons a day of corn likker, strong enough to fire up a tractor. What with corn sellin' for three cents a bushel, he ain't hurtin'. Says he's gonna buy a bigger truck. The one he's drivin' now is only four years old. It's in top shape and looks good, but it's too small for the long haul. Then he's got twenty head of cattle and, of course, hogs. His well runs dry by late spring and for years he's been using mine. I've got the best well in the county and frontage on the Lost River where our pastures adjoin. He's heard I'm thinkin' about leavin' and that's stirred him up to make an offer. He needs my water bad.

"Seven hundred dollars for forty acres. Whaddaya think? Has he watered it?"

"Of course, but if you're hell bent to do this, tell him to throw in the truck and it's a go. Hold his feet to the fire and he'll deal."

"I won't know what to do with all that money and a good-lookin' truck too."

"For starters, get yourself a haircut and some decent clothes and stick around a week or so and get yourself sorted out. You wouldn't be a bad-looking fellow if you were shined up a little."

"Might just do that. Thanks, Fritz. See you tomorrow."

Business was slow so I closed the bar early and went home.

"Hey, Bessie, light of my life. I'm home. Um, do I smell apple pie? Nobody makes an apple pie that compares to yours."

"I know, but don't tell Helga."

"Helmer and I had a long talk today. He's decided to sell his property and move to North Dakota. I wasn't able to talk him out of that crazy idea. I feel really bad about that and I'll hate to see him go. Bjournson made him an offer that I have advised him on and I think we have that straightened out."

"I know. I heard it on the party line. Bjournson is bragging how he got the best of the deal."

"Well, long live the party line. Stay tuned and you'll probably hear he's been premature. Helmer hasn't got much book-learning, but he's got a world of common sense and he's dead honest. He's been helping Olaf and me put together the proposal for a charter to organize this town and keep it that way. He'd be an asset, and we need all the good men we can find. I have a strong feeling he's off the booze for good and he's going to make it this time. I'll be sorry if it's someplace else. This town will lose a good man, and Helga will be the biggest loser of all. I wish this story had a happy ending."

"Fritz, you know the Torgersons have been the pillar of

responsibility in this community for generations. Helga has a lot of pride. I should know—she's my best friend."

"Pride? How long does it take 'pride' to melt into just plain bullheadedness?"

"Before you get on your soapbox, Fritz, let me tell you something I've been thinking about. Now listen.

"I know Helga cares for Helmer or I wouldn't interfere. She's kept him around for thirty years. You know those Norwegians are a clannish bunch. He's not in, but he's never out, either. Now if Helga thought he was interested in another woman, I can promise you she'd come out of her corner with the gloves on. Here is the perfect opportunity and, with a little effort, a possible solution to both your problems."

"Bessie at her best—on her own soapbox."

She laughed and said, "Step back and just listen! The Ladies' Aid Society is putting on a box social next week to raise money for the addition of a classroom."

"Box social? Is that the same as a basket social?"

"Yes. The women pack a fancy lunch, add a pie, and put everything in a box all prettied up to be auctioned off. Supposedly no one knows what box belongs to who, but, of course, the whispers and hints have made the rounds and generally everyone lunches with the person of their choice. Purely a fun event, even when it gets competitive, and many a romance has been sparked there.

"Everyone is enjoying the party and could enjoy it more, but the pastor won't permit dancing or cards in the church basement. So there goes the whist—will you gentlemen be bored?

"As the new president of the Ladies' Aid Society, I happen

to know Inga Torvig has a purple basket with big pink ribbons and bows all over it—sure can't miss it. She's been a widow for years and Lars has been courting her for years. But he's slow on the draw, so Helmer can—*must*—buy Inga's basket and act like he's having a wonderful time when he shares it with her. And, of course, he'll take her home. He must not let anyone outbid him, no matter how high it goes. I guarantee he will have Helga's full attention. It's up to him what he'll do with it."

"Bessie, my love, I think it could work. Your beauty and my brains—how did I get so lucky?"

She ignored my feeble attempt at humor.

"What's that awful noise?" she interrupted, looking out the window. "Oh, someone is leaning on the horn. Looks like Bjournson's pickup."

"It *was* Bjournson's—now it's Helmer's," I answered. "We're going to Thief River Falls to do some paperwork and some shopping. I could use a good haircut too. I'll run your plan past Helmer. Hope I can talk him into it—it's sure worth a try. See you later, my love."

Not a week later, dressed in our best, we nudged our way into the crowded church basement.

"Well, Bessie, this is the day the trap is sprung. Are we ready?"

"Shhh, hush your mouth, Fritz. Do you have to tell the whole world? Look for a good seat. What a crowd—biggest we've ever had. Looks like the whole county is here. Folks really want that new schoolroom. Is this the quietest seat you could find? There are the Melbys, the Torgersons, and look, there's Helmer. He looks downright handsome."

I turned to see him talking and laughing with a group of fellows, with his shoulders back and his head up. It was obvious he was enjoying himself. I marveled at this transformation brought about by a decent pair of pants with a few bucks in the pocket, a white shirt, and a good haircut.

Looking around, I saw the colorful boxes laid neatly on long tables covered with white cloth that showed them to full advantage. I spotted Inga's box immediately and hoped Helmer had seen it too. His future was riding on that cardboard.

The young fellows were stampeding around, shamelessly showing off in front of the girls who pretended total indifference. We older folks just enjoyed the show and remembered when.

Then the auctioneer waved, quieting the crowd.

"How-de-do, folks. This looks like a happy, prosperous gathering and for such a good cause. Be generous and we'll add two rooms to the school. Aren't these boxes beautiful? Each of them contains a wonderful lunch and, I've been told, fresh apple pie right out of the oven. Now folks, it's for your children, so dig deep and be generous.

"I'm gonna start with this lovely green and yellow box. Will you look at these ribbons? How long did it take some lady to make it? I can smell that pie. Be generous and you will taste it.

"What am I bid? Let's start at a dollar fifty. C'mon, folks. Gimme seventy-five, seventy-five. Gimme sixty-five. It's for your first graders."

He was pacing back and forth, holding the box high. A hand flew up and he bellows, "Going for sixty-five. Going, going, gone to the young man sitting with the pretty girl in the blue dress."

I looked over to see Ila and Billy Swensen.

Then the bidding grew fast and furious. The noise was deafening.

"Now you folks have caught the vision," the auctioneer whooped and held the boxes higher still.

I was so distracted, I almost missed Bessie's creation, but I was reminded at the last moment by a nudge that almost broke my rib, but saved Bessie from Bjournson's effort to outbid me on my own wife's basket.

When Helga's box came up, Helmer was seemingly in deep conversation and didn't notice when Bjournson carried her box and seated himself beside her. I could feel her bristle from across the room.

Bessie muttered, "She's not pleased." A fact I could plainly see.

When the auctioneer held Inga's box up, my heart started to pound and I could feel the sweat beneath my collar. I looked at Bessie, her face as calm as though she was seated in the front pew.

Where was Helmer? *C'mon, Helmer, don't fail me now or we'll both have to leave town.* He turned and smiled at me as if I had called his name.

The auctioneer was pleading for a fifty-cent bid. Lars offered twenty-five, Helmer called thirty. A few scattered efforts from the crowd brought the bid to sixty.

Then it was just Lars and Helmer. Lars was always the low bidder, but he was persistent. My worry climbed to new heights. I nudged Bessie for a little encouragement, but she didn't seem to notice. Then the rivalry became apparent to the crowd and the room reverberated with whistling and clapping and words of encouragement for both contestants.

Lars bid one dollar and looked pleased with himself.

Helmer stood, laughing, and waved a five-dollar bill. Lars looked disgusted, threw up his hands, and sat down as the crowd erupted.

Bessie sat with her hands over her ears and watched as Helmer carried the purple box with the long pink ribbons floating triumphantly behind, sat down with a blushing, laughing Inga as she cut the pie.

I dared glance at Helga. Her face was like a thundercloud. She sliced her pie with such energy you'd think she was cutting the head off a chicken. I was glad it was Bjournson who was sitting beside her.

CHAPTER 17

"G'morning, Ma."

"You're early, son."

"Yes, it's time I got back on the job. Where's Orren?"

"He must have gone already. I haven't seen him. Bessie called to say the social brought in over thirty dollars."

"I bet it was Unk's five that put it over the top."

"I must say I was pleased to see you and Marguerite having such a good time. You whisked her away from that other fellow on the second bid."

"Anything to make you happy, Ma. Appeared Unk did a little whisking too. He sure was enjoying himself and didn't he look good?"

"No, he did not. He made such a spectacle of himself, everybody's talking. Lars has been keeping company with Inga for going on three years. They're practically engaged."

"Well, Ma, maybe Unk built a fire under him. Inga must be tired of waiting. She's been a widow too long. Helmer could do worse. She's a nice little woman, owns her own place…"

"Olaf, I don't want to talk about Helmer."

"Ma, why don't you give him a break? Doesn't it mean anything to you that he saved my life? And nobody has ever worked harder on this farm. You know he loves you, but don't expect him to wait forever."

"I won't condone his drinking and now he's disgraced himself by slipping around with another man's woman. I felt sorry for Lars."

"In case you haven't noticed, Ma, Helmer has sworn off."

"Again?"

"Why not? Has change ever been easy for anybody? Give him another chance, Ma, and what about you? Don't you ever get tired of living just for us? Don't you deserve more? You're barely fifty years old. There's a lot of years ahead of you, so why don't you spend it with someone you love? Better think about it, Ma. I'm inviting Helmer for supper and you better mind your manners."

"Olaf, will you stop that foolish talk and answer the phone?"

"Here, Ma, it's the pastor."

"Good morning, Mrs. Torgerson. I am sorry to bring this disturbing news to you so early in the morning, but I just received a phone call from my daughter in St. Paul informing me she is celebrating her eighteenth birthday as Mrs. Orren Torgerson. They must have slipped away right after prayers."

"Pastor, I had no idea!"

"I am not as upset about it as I could be because the Good Book says it is better to marry than to burn, and things certainly seemed to be heating up at an alarming rate. Your son is very headstrong, Mrs. Torgerson."

"Yes, and it seems your daughter is keeping up very nicely."

"Well, yes, maybe so. We will have some festivities when they get back. My daughter says Orren has rented a suite at a fine hotel and they will be back when his money runs out."

"That shouldn't take long, Pastor. I'll put the coffee on."

"Hi, Unk, I'm inviting you to supper for Baby Doll's birthday party. Fried chicken, mashed potatoes, and I saw with my own eyes thirteen egg whites go into that angel food cake. Ma had to lock the boys outside when she frosted it."

"Olaf, you're inviting me to my own execution. You know, she hasn't even wasted a hello on me all these weeks."

"I know. Maybe we can soften her up. I want to see you where you belong—right where she wants you to be if she'd admit it. C'mon, what have you got to lose?"

"Can't I beg off?"

"No. Don't make me put the cuffs on."

CHAPTER 18

When the door pushed open, I didn't need to look. I put the towel down and started the coffee.

"Helmer, where in hell have you been? It's been three days since the box social and Bessie and I have been holding our breath, waiting to hear what happened."

"We got married, that's what happened."

"I'll be damned. I didn't know you were such a fast talker. Married? Honestly?"

"By the pastor himself. Don't I look married?"

"Well, you look awfully pleased with yourself. Bessie will be so thrilled. Hell, I'm thrilled."

"Fritz, save your hugs for Bessie—yer breakin' my ribs. I wanted you to be the first to know since you and Bessie hatched up this scheme that has made me the happiest man."

"Don't keep me in suspense, damn it. What happened at the birthday party?"

"I'm tryin' to tell you if you'll just calm down. Pour yerself a cuppa coffee and set back."

I poured. Helmer made himself comfortable, lightened the sugar bowl by four cubes, and blew on his coffee before he began.

"I had just finished milkin' when I looked to see Olaf waitin'. We walked to the house together. Helga gave me an icy hello and I figgered I'd got off easy. The supper wuz everything Olaf promised. The cake seemed a foot high and the four pink candles flickered as Buddy took his chances with the wooden spoon and tested the frosting with a stubby finger. He thought nobody wuz lookin' but, of course, we were all watchin' Olaf as he held Baby Doll and fed her from his own plate. Marguerite shook her head, but she wuz laughing as she made sure everyone had second helpings.

"The candles were burning low when Helga said, 'Son, you lit the candles too soon.'

" 'No, she wanted to see them burn. Anything my birthday girl wants.'

"There wuz such love in this big strong man's voice that I kept my eyes on my fork to hide the tears that threatened to betray me.

"The candles sputtered as Baby tried to blow them out without much luck. Olaf tried to wipe the spit bubbles from her tiny chin, but she hid her face in his clean shirt and I could tell he never noticed or would have cared.

"The boys were beggin' to help until Olaf, with one puff, left only the smoke. Then he held the tiny, sticky hand in his big fist and together they cut the birthday cake. Nobody seemed to notice the frosting wuz thin on the side that faced Buddy's plate.

"Fritz, you shoulda seen that cake. And it tasted as good as it looked."

"So you survived the dinner?"

"Yeah, but I could feel I wuzn't home free. When the party wuz over Marguerite carried the baby to bed. Olaf stood and said, 'C'mon boys, we've got time for a coupla games of checkers.' When the boys left, Olaf said, 'Stick around, Unk, and I'll beat you at a game of whist.' After that it wuz just Helga, me, and the dishes. I tried to make my escape, but she tossed the dish towel at me and said, 'Here, you can pay for your supper.'

"I said, 'Certainly, it wuz a wonderful meal and I enjoyed every bite of that birthday cake.' I had been hopin' to slide by on that, but no such luck. Helga asked, 'Did you enjoy it as much as the pie with the burnt crust that you squandered five dollars on?'

" 'Wuz it burnt? I never noticed.'

" 'No, you were too busy being the life of the party. You should be ashamed. Everybody's talking about you and that little fat Inga.'

" 'Fat? I thought she wuz just pleasingly plump.'

" 'Yes, like a pillow tied in the middle, and anybody can see she dyes her hair. Once at Ladies' Aid, I smelled smoke on her. I think she rolls her own. Bull Durham, no doubt.'

" 'Well, it's nice to know she's economical. She's easy to pass the time of day with too, and owns her little farm. Keeps it neat as a pin. She's affectionate too. I gave her a little squeeze when I helped her out of the truck and she invited me in for coffee.'

"Fritz, I know I wuz gettin' in deep, but, like you said, what did I have to lose? Her face flushed red and I knew I'd touched a nerve."

"Helmer, I can't tell you how this conversation bores me. You go home. Go on, go home."

"With that, the wet soapy dishrag caught me right across the face without even thinking, I flipped her with the end of the dish towel right where her dress gets tight when she bends over, and I meant for it to sting.

" 'Now I'll get the rest of my stuff and I won't bother you again—that's a promise,' I told her and stomped off to the bunkhouse to pick up my things and throw them in the back of the truck. When I opened the door, she wuz just sittin' there with tears streamin' down her face.

" 'Helga, you'll have to move. I'm going home.'

" 'Helmer, you are home.' She moved against me…. Okay, Fritz, I can't begin to tell you…."

"You can't stop now, Helmer!"

He looked at me and continued. " 'Move over,' I said and shifted into high gear.

"The pastor came to the door, stuffing his nightshirt into his pants. He didn't seem happy to see us.

" 'My goodness, couldn't this wait till morning?'

" 'No,' I told him, 'I've waited thirty years.'

"So we were married. Me in my barn clothes, Helga in her apron. When we got back, I parked in front of the bunkhouse and she ast, 'Surely you don't expect me to sleep in the bunkhouse, do you?'

" 'You won't notice the clutter, I promise,' I told her.

"I carried her over the threshold and when I put her down, she said, 'You remember where you flipped me with that towel? That really stung, so now you can kiss it and make it better.'

" 'What better way to start,' I said and kicked the door shut.

"The next morning, Marguerite said, 'Where's Ma? Her bed hasn't been slept in.'

"Olaf wuz laughing so hard he could only point."

CHAPTER 19

I had just finished the last of the glasses and tossed the bar towel when Helmer walked in. It took my senses a minute to register, to recognize this tall, handsome man with a confident walk, clear eyes sparkling with the joy of living, and radiating happiness.

"Helmer! Thought your honeymoon must have done you in. It's been awhile since you've been in. See—the door is still on the hinges. How are you?"

"Couldn't be better, Fritz, and I have you and yer wife to thank. I'm gonna name the firstborn after you."

"C'mon, Helmer. Mrs. Melby says…."

"Fritz, has that damn woman been talkin' to yer wife too? Helga is too sensible to listen to that, I'll tell you. She don't pay her no mind, so don't give up hope fer a namesake. We're workin' on it."

We laughed and speculated on Mrs. Melby's needs as I put on a fresh pot and pulled up a stool.

"Well, what else is new? I don't hear any of the good stuff

when you're not around."

I poured us a cup and he said, "Have you heard Olaf is goin' up to Lake of the Woods for the last fishin' trip before the ice? Just gonna be gone over the Halloween weekend. Marguerite and Baby Doll are goin' too, and Helga is gonna tag along. She loves to fish, so I guess I can spare her for a coupla days. Olaf says he's gonna learn Marguerite how to fish, but it looks to me like she's already caught the big one. Sure glad he took the bait. He couldn't have found a better one, or one as purty. Me 'n Ila are gonna stay home, keep the boys, and tend to the chores. Ila doesn't want to go—I don't think she's got fishin' on her mind. She plans to make Halloween costumes for the boys and take 'em to town for a while, and I'd guess enjoy a little Halloween with the Swenson boy. Olaf will be busy with the sheriffin' when he gets back, and I'll be awful busy at the farm now that Orren is gone."

"Orren gone? Gone where? He just got married. Has the party line gone dead? Haven't heard a word."

"You haven't heard Orren has gone to the seminary? Studyin' to be a preacher. Can you believe that? A preacher!"

"Hell, no. Not a preacher—not in a million years."

"Well, believe this. The pastor's cook has a purty daughter who seems to have been puttin' on weight lately, most in front. Turns out she's 'bout four months gone. The pastor paid for her ticket to Californy where she's gonna stay with kinfolk fer a spell. Then the pastor held a gun on Orren and gave him a choice. I heard it wuz an easy one—the seminary or the hereafter.

"Don't doubt it wuz an easy decision. I sure as hell wouldn't want to irritate that old bible-thumper with the Good Book in one hand and his shotgun in the other.

"Orren jist danced right into Thief River Falls and signed up at the seminary. Lotta folks gonna be surprised to see him in the pulpit.

"Can't say the pastor ain't a fair man.

"Fritz, I gotta go. Don't want to git behind on my honeymoonin'. See ya later."

The door had hardly closed behind him when it was flung open and Helmer hurried back in.

"Fritz, Fritz! Is yer house still fer sale? Tell me you haven't sold that house."

"Hell, no, I haven't sold it. The signs have been up all summer and not one bite."

"Well, it's sold now! You know I've got the money. Let's shake on it! I'll be so proud to give Helga that house for a wedding present. She's always said it wuz the prettiest house in town. When can we move in?"

"Wait just a minute! I've got to break this news to Bessie. We'll move just as soon as we can decide where. You know, Bessie has wanted to go back to the city and I've promised. But damn, I'll hate to leave!"

CHAPTER 20

A few days later, I finished work early. Thought I could clean up tomorrow.

"Bessie, I'm home. Where are you? I've got great news and a surprise that's going to make you happy. Helmer was in and we talked for an hour. He's the happiest man I've ever seen. Now for the surprise…"

"No, no, me first. I want to tell you my surprise that will make you happier than Helmer."

"That will be hard to do, my love."

"Fritz, I've changed my mind about moving. I realize how deeply you are involved in the rebirth of this little town. I see how you and Olaf have laid the plans and how it's all coming together. I know how much that means to you."

"Bessie…"

"Don't interrupt. You've been asked to serve as the school principal, and Helga tells me that Olaf wants you on the town council. This town needs us. Me too, now that I've been voted president of the Ladies' Aid. At last I'm comfortable here and

I don't want to move."

"Bessie, will you let me finish? It's too late, Bessie. We have to move. I just sold this house."

"You sold my house? You couldn't have done that—this is a very poor joke."

"No joke, Bessie. I've got a check in my pocket."

"I hate you, Fritz! Don't touch me—how could you? How could you do this to me?"

"Bessie, be reasonable. Don't cry. Didn't we have a discussion about selling this house last spring? As I remember, I lost weight on Mrs. Melby's soup diet. And now suddenly you've changed your mind? Damn it to hell—will anybody ever figure out a woman's mind? I wanted to surprise you. I knew you'd be so happy to hear it."

"Well, I'm certainly surprised," she said, with ice dripping from her words.

"Bessie, I've given my word and shook on it. I believe you made it plain—your exact words: 'not much of a man who doesn't keep his word.' Now what do you expect me to do? Will you open this door? Please open the door. Don't cry, you know I can't stand that."

But Bessie's stance never softened.

"Bessie, it's been over a week and Mrs. Melby's soup is going to be the death of me," I pleaded.

"What did you expect when you turned me out of my own house? Did you think I'd be overjoyed to sleep in some ratty place with bedbugs while you were looking for another house? You've broken my heart with your irrational actions."

"Be reasonable, Bessie You know it was you who wanted to move." I tried in vain to defend myself.

"Where in the world did you get that idea? Why would I want to move?"

"Please stop crying, Bessie. Here's my hankie. Blow your nose and let's discuss this rationally. You know I'd do anything for you. Hell, someday I'll even build you a house just the way you want it. Big windows, a bathroom. Please don't cry. Oh, and a kitchen like you've always wanted."

"You'll build me a house? Oh, Fritz, I love you. Just the way I want it? My dream house," she cried as she flung her arms around my neck.

"Well, well, I guess I would someday, maybe. I'll sure think about it."

"Time's up! You've thought about it. You can buy that big lot next door—it's been for sale for years. The house of my dreams," she enthused. "I can just see it—big windows, bigger rooms, an indoor bathroom. I'd have more room for my flower garden. Oh, Fritz, I do love you. Let's draw the plans tomorrow. It's bedtime now."

"Bessie, I only said maybe. Give me some time to think." But there was no escaping.

"If you need time to think, do it at Mrs. Melby's when you get your soup."

"Bessie, if Mrs. Melby's soup doesn't kill me, this woof-woof three times a week is going to cut my life short. Three times a week—Bessie, have mercy!"

"C'mon, Fritz. Woof-woof!"

She threw her arms around me, I blew out the light, and then it was woof-woof.

The next morning I'd hardly pulled my pants on when the phone rang.

Damn that phone. Only Helga would call this early. I could plan on breakfast being late.

Bessie picked up the phone in the kitchen. That was a good sign—maybe the coffee would be perked.

I could hear Helga's jubilant voice as I finished dressing.

"Oh, Bessie, I'm so happy. Helmer has just given me this wonderful news! You know I've always loved your house and now to know it's mine. Helmer says it's my wedding present!

"You know this has happened at just the right time. Ila wants to be in town for her senior year, close to her friends and class activities. I've worried so about Buddy starting first grade in that drafty little country schoolhouse. He would have a cold all winter."

"What? Your voice sounds funny, Bessie—do you have a cold?"

Then they both sounded like pneumonia had just set in. Later, I heard all about Helga's vegetable garden and knew exactly where Bessie's pansies would be planted.

Breakfast was delayed, of course. I was late to open up again, but I generously conceded it was a small price to pay.

Bessie's plans were drawn on the back of a kitchen napkin and there would be no doubt as to what she wanted and intended to have.

After the shock had worn off, I was caught up in her joy and swept along in her enthusiasm.

Supplies rolled in, and the bangs of hammers and the squeal of saws that resounded from daylight to dark competed with the jokes and raucous laughter of the eight-man crew that Olaf had put together.

Helga and Bessie had outdone themselves with a hot

dinner and steaming coffee at straight-up twelve noon, plus better-than-average wages gave the workplace a festive air.

Then, too, Bessie's offer of a twenty-five-dollar bonus, to be shared among the men if the plumbing was in before the big freeze, got instant consideration. Somehow I wasn't surprised to see the pipes sticking up almost before the foundation was in.

Helmer and I stood back and watched with a mixture of awe and delight to see our wives take command of the building project. We concluded that we had never seen them so happy.

Both Helmer and myself enjoyed the side benefits.

CHAPTER 21

Reluctantly, the last summer days faded and grew short. The trees looked naked without their leaves, which scattered about in the gusty wind.

Folks were getting ready for winter's onslaught, putting up storm windows to keep the cold out, tar papering the foundation to keep the heat from escaping, filling the woodshed to capacity.

Kids were planning for Halloween and, now that great day had arrived, there were witches on their mother's broomsticks with black hats flapping and goblins and white-sheeted ghosts with baskets at the ready. Shrieks and laughter sounded from everywhere as they prowled the streets.

Oh, yes, make no mistake—Halloween was here. With that came Frankie and Buddy.

"Fritz, what in the world are you doing? Are you sick? It's three o'clock. Come to bed for goodness sake. Has Halloween done you in?"

"No, I'm not sick, not yet. I can't sleep."

"Well, that doesn't surprise me. Sitting in a kitchen chair drinking coffee doesn't help much. What's the trouble? You look terrible."

"Nothing, I told you. Go back to bed, Bessie. I need to think."

"I'll just sit awhile with you. You're upset, I can tell. Have some trouble at the bar?"

"Not trouble, I hope."

"Fritz, tell me. Come on—trouble, isn't it."

"No, well, maybe…yes. I know where Charbeneau is."

"Has he come back at last?"

"I'd say he's back for sure."

Bessie turned the lamp up and complained, "When in the world are we going to get electricity in here?"

When I just sat there, my head in my hands, she pulled her chair closer and took my hand in hers. "Come on, honey, you know you can tell me."

I didn't know where to start.

"Go to bed, Bessie, so I can think."

"Since when haven't we always confided in each other. After fifty years, what's changed?"

"All right, all right. Put on another pot."

It was hard to find the words to start, but then the gate opened and the story flooded out.

"Although it was early, tonight was pretty crowded. Halloween, you know. Around seven, I'd guess, the CCC boys were in and having a good time. Some farmer came in wearing a mask made out of turkey feathers, said his wife made it. You can believe the boys were having fun with that.

Then, of course, the bar was lined, the regulars rolling dice to see who was paying for the drinks and arguing politics. It was thick with smoke and noisy as usual.

"I had everybody taken care of and was mixing myself a little reinforcement when I looked up to see two little white-sheeted ghosts pushing and laughing in the half-opened doorway. I recognized Buddy Torgerson and his pal, Frankie. Swinging between them was a human skull. 'Trick or treat, mister,' they whooped, and swung it high. I saw it was suspended by a faded red and black rag stuffed through the eye sockets. Faded as it was, instinctively I knew it was a remnant from the mackinaw that Charbeneau had worn the morning he left for St. Louis. A patch of black hair seemed to be embedded in the thing they swung with such enthusiasm.

"Fritz, Fritz, stop! I'm going to faint."

"Damn it to hell, Bessie, you have to know everything, so sit down and shut up.

"I shot a look around that smoky room, turkey feathers everywhere. Nobody even looked up when I hurried the boys behind the bar. Instinctively I knew. I knew Charbeneau had never made it to St. Paul.

"That knowledge hit me in the solar plexus like a giant fist. My heart pounded so badly I thought I was having an attack. My stomach sickened and a sour taste filled my mouth. When I could talk, I asked, 'Where did you boys find this ugly thing?'

" 'Way out behind the feed shed,' Frankie said. 'You know, where my dad kept that mean old pig.'

"Then I knew I was going to be sick.

" 'Boys, will you wait a minute? I'll be right back. I think we can make a deal.'

"I made a run for it, but lost the race at the door. Lars was shooting craps at the bar, but he turned around and said, 'Geez, Fritz, you don't look so good. I'll clean that mess up for you—probably need the practice. Knute and me are gonna go pardners and buy this place. Still for sale, ain't it?' I could only nod.

"I washed my face and went back. 'Do your mothers know about this? Have you showed this to anyone besides me?'

" 'No, we wuz gonna surprise 'em when they came back from fishin' so I hid it under my sheet so Ila couldn't see it when she brung us to town.' Buddy laughed and said, 'Huh, Frankie?' and he nodded.

"Now don't interrupt me, Bessie. I'm trying to get this out. So then I said, 'Tell you what, men. Here's a dollar for each of you and two bags—big bags, see?—of jelly beans. And I'll throw in a couple of Hershey bars. Trade you for that dirty old thing and you won't have to carry it around. You'd be in trouble if your mothers saw it, and I'd hate to think what Ila would do. How about it, men? Is it a deal? Shake on it. Let's keep this a secret just between you and me, okay?

"Now what the hell am I going to do with that skull?' "

"Honey, let me warm up your coffee. Tell me everything. What do you think happened? How did he get into that boar pen?"

"I think Olaf, and Orren too, caught up with him somewhere along the highway and done him in. Then they brought him home and threw him in with that boar. They figured that would take care of the evidence. It would have too, if it hadn't been for those kids. It was a hell of a way to go, even for Charbeneau."

"There had to be more to it than that, Fritz. How did all this happen?"

"Well, Charbeneau came in early to get a bottle to take with him to St. Paul. The Torgersons got in from that fishing trip, I'd say, an hour or so afterwards and stopped for a drink before they went on home. I'm thinking they were on the road as soon as they saw their little brother's broken nose and their sister all bandaged up with her hair cut off. I don't want to think about what happened when they caught him."

"Oh, Fritz, I can't believe that. Not Orren, not Olaf."

"Believe it. Those Torgerson men have scary tempers. I've seen them clear out the bar in a matter of minutes when they got riled. Charbeneau was living on borrowed time."

"Well, I don't believe it. No, I don't."

"Bessie, what would you believe? Give me a clue."

"Well, he was probably drinking as he drove. You said he took a bottle with him. He was tired, drunk, and confused, and he just turned around and came home. Then he went down to check on his boar and just fell in. See? An accident."

"Bessie, that damn boar wasn't even home yet and you know damn well that Olaf did him in, then brought that boar back. You'll remember they brought him back three days after Charbeneau supposedly went to St. Paul."

"Yes, of course they brought him back. They're honest men and they had only borrowed him."

"They kept him for over four months, that's what caused all the trouble, so why did they hurry to bring him home three days after Charbeneau left? I'll tell you why. They needed him and not for breeding. That's why. Face up to it, Bessie."

"You! You yourself said he needed to be hung."

"Yes, but to be beaten to death and fed to a hog…."

She put her arms around me and said, "Fritz, why are you making such a case against Olaf? You've been as close to him as if he were your son."

"God knows I don't want to hurt him. I do love him like a son, but my conscience—how can I live with that?"

"Fritz, listen to me! Helga confided to me that he and Marguerite are going to get married in church at Christmas time. She and I are already planning the reception. You know she's my dearest friend. Look how she's kept that farm going all these years and raised her family. You've wondered how Olaf, and Orren too, is so well spoken, so far advanced, so different from the rest of the men. I tell you it's because of Helga's sacrifice, her efforts. She kept the farm alone every winter so the boys could go to the best school in Thief River for an education. Now she has her chance for happiness. Consider that. The Torgersons have lived here for generations. Grandpa Gunther built the church, laid the foundation for the school and gave the money to build it. He canceled the loan on Melby's store when the widow couldn't make the payments. Who are you to destroy that family? Look at what Olaf has accomplished and you've helped him. You and he have worked side by side to make this town what it is today. Would you throw all that away for a dead man? Your 'conscience' would tear this town apart. I say to hell with your conscience!"

"Well, Bessie, what am I going to do?"

She moved to put her arm around me and said, "I don't understand. You're not involved."

"Hell, yes, I'm involved, and now that I know, I'll have to testify in court. God knows I don't want to…." My voice broke and I pulled away from Bessie. Putting my head in my hands, I wanted to cry like a baby. The realization of how the coming events would play out sickened me.

The frightening thought rushed like an avalanche through my mind and I started to shake. Bessie said, "You'd testify against Olaf? Then I'd have to testify against you."

"How could you? Don't talk foolish, Bessie."

"I'll say you came home blind drunk and I had to put you to bed."

"For God's sake, you wouldn't, Bessie!"

"Don't try me—don't. Where is that thing?"

"In the car, hidden inside a gunny sack."

"Give me the keys."

"Bessie, you don't want to see that."

"Yes, I do. Where is the flashlight? Here, have a cup of coffee. I'll be right back."

It seemed like hours later when she reappeared. I said, "What took you so long? I've about drained the coffeepot."

She stood there, with hands on hips, and said, "You should stick to coffee, you and your 'reinforced' drink. You've created a tempest in a teapot."

"How did Shakespeare get into this conversation? Say what you mean."

"I mean that you're stirring up a lot of trouble for nothing. Anyone with normal vision can plainly see that the object you've made such a fuss about is only a Halloween basket shaped like a skull, made out of papier maché and painted white. I can't believe you thought it was real and let your imagination run away with you. Don't let your mind dwell on such ridiculous things. Maybe you need to get your glasses checked. I'll make an appointment for you."

"But, Bessie…."

"I suppose it looked kind of real, but when I looked closely, it was plain to see it was only papier maché. I know artificial flowers are made of that and they look so real a person can almost smell the fragrance. See, you've worried yourself for nothing. People would want to put you away if you expected them to believe that old thing was real. Don't embarrass yourself, Fritz. I'll bury it in the root cellar if it will make you feel better."

A wild hope flashed through my mind. I wiped my face and considered that possibility. Surely it could have happened that way. What a reasonable solution to this unbearable position.

"Well, Bessie, now that I put my mind to it, I know that the lighting is poor down there—I've been meaning to get new bulbs. And I'd probably had a few drinks with the regulars too—all that Halloween foolishness. You know I was awfully tired, having been on my feet for hours—and all that noise. Sometimes I do get a little scattered. Hell, I can't find my glasses half the time. Guess I must have been a little tipsy and just got a silly notion like you said—probably had the DTs before I got drunk. Ha ha! Suppose I won't sleep a wink after all that coffee."

"Sleep? It's almost six o'clock. I'll give you a little breakfast."

"No, no, just a cup of coffee. I'm going back down—there's always something to do. I'm thinking it's going to be an interesting day."

"Fritz, do you think Olaf will be in?"

"I don't doubt he'll be waiting at the door, Bessie. I'm going down now."

"Fritz, promise me you won't—listen to me! You know we discussed everything last night."

"Bessie, let me go. I'll tell you everything when I get home. Old folks need their sleep and I'm feeling older than Methuselah this morning. Yes, yes, I'll be home early. Will you please let me say goodbye?"

"Fritz, remember what we talked…."

"I'll talk to you later, Bessie."

Bessie's suggestion, which I had clung to in the dark of night, dissolved with the first light that lit the way.

I drove down to the bar slowly, my mind in turmoil, my conscience a battlefield upon which waged a war that took no prisoners with the grim consequences of my decision.

My love and respect, along with my silence, was all that guaranteed Olaf's future and that of the entire Torgerson family.

The sweat ran down in little rivulets and dampened my collar as my heart pounded with every breath. From a block away, I could see his pickup parked at the curb. He was waiting, as I knew he would be, at the door. Silently, I prayed for both of us—prayed I would make the right decision and that he would understand.

I parked beside him.

"You're out early, Olaf."

"Yes, just happened by on my way to see a couple of farmers fighting over a fence line."

"People can sure get emotional over a fence line," I acknowledged. "Come on in and have a cup of coffee."

He rolled a cigarette took a puff, then snubbed it out.

"Thought you quit smoking, Olaf."

"I did. The baby said I smelled nasty."

The small talk faltered, his eyes met mine unblinkingly, and he cut right to the chase.

"My little brother tells me he got the best of you in a business deal on Halloween. That right?"

"Sure did. He and his pal came in carrying an old skull that looked like it had seen better days. They were swinging it between them suspended by a dirty red and black rag. I just talked them out of it—figured their mothers wouldn't approve of them carrying it all over town."

"Well, I sure appreciate that," he said, and started to roll another smoke, but his hand shook and the tobacco spilled so he tossed it.

"Did they say where they found it?"

"Yes, said it was down in Charbeneau's old pigpen behind the feed shed."

I gave it to him straight. His eyes met mine and the naked truth lay bare between us. Pulsing down his suddenly white face, that scar seemed as if it had been drawn by a child's red crayon. His voice shook as he asked, "What are you going to do with it, Fritz?"

"I don't know," I answered.

I waited while he fumbled with a cigarette.

Then he said, "I heard some farmer from Bemidji bought Charbeneau's property from the bank when they foreclosed, and he's plowed up all the old pastures to put in his winter wheat. Did you know this part of Minnesota used to belong to the Mandan Indians—it was their camping grounds. That farmer probably plowed up their old burial place."

"You know Frankie and Buddy—they play cowboys and

Indians all over hell's half acre."

Our eyes locked; Olaf seemed to force his next words.

"Hard to tell where they found that skull, wouldn't you say?"

The silence hung thick between us for what seemed like an eternity. Then I heard a voice from somewhere answer, "Seems logical to me, Olaf."

His eyes closed for a long moment. He opened his lips as if to speak, but no sounds came for a while.

"What did you do with that thing?"

"I put it in a gunnysack and stashed it in the trunk of my car. I don't know what in hell to do with it. Could you get rid of it for me? I'd sure appreciate it, Olaf."

"He sat quiet took a few deep drags from that cigarette, then nodded. I tossed him the keys and he caught them in midair, then stubbed out his cigarette. I poured him a double shot. As he knocked it back with one gulp, I saw the color flood back in his face, the scar pale, and his hands stop shaking.

I walked with him to the door, waited as he opened the trunk, and watched as he drove away with that gunnysack that held his salvation.

For the first time in my life, I felt old. Old and empty. A smothering wave of mixed emotions swept over me as I leaned into the door jam, fighting for breath. I closed my eyes and pulled the door shut behind me.

I started to walk, my feet taking their own direction on the new sidewalk. Passing Melby's, I saw myself reflected in the big windows of the new storefront. Two doors down, it was Sorenson's Pool Hall that shined like new with its fresh coat of paint. The gas station now boasted another pump, and nearby I noticed a new street light.

The whining sound of a high-pitched saw caught my attention, and then I heard the pounding hammers. I looked to see the framework of the new room for first graders snugged up against the old schoolhouse. I knew this was Bessie's Ladies' Aid contribution from their numerous bake sales. My gaze wandered to the playground where the paint was still shiny-new on the slides and swings. I knew they wouldn't look new very long.

The weathered steeple on the Lutheran church was gone. In its place was an ornate spire that pointed to the heavens—I recognized the pastor's efforts.

From somewhere came the sure knowledge that I had made the right decision—that certainty took root and flowered and I had peace of mind. My heart rejoiced, my steps lengthened as I turned back. I knew Bessie would be waiting.

She met me at the door.

"Fritz! You're home—it isn't even noon. You must have smelled this apple pie. Tell me everything!"

"Yes, I just locked the damn door and came home. I'll tell you everything, then never, never! mention it again. Promise?"

Finally, the pie was gone like yesterday, peace was wrapped around me like a warm blanket, and tomorrow is another day.

CHAPTER 22

"Well, Helmer, is the honeymoon going to last forever? It's been two months since you lovebirds tied the knot. Still honeymooning?"

"Fer sure. This honeymoon is gonna last forever and we're honeymoonin' in the big house now. Helga says I catch her too easy in the bunkhouse, but I notice I don't have any trouble catchin' her anywhere.

"But the big house seems crowded. She's countin' the days till we get moved. How soon will your house be finished? Spose you've got a good crew. Eight men, it should go up quick…."

"Not quick enough to suit those two women. The kitchen and bathroom are done and we're finishing up on the bedroom. Bessie wants Helga to be able to move in by Christmas—our Christmas present to you both. We can get along just fine with our new bedroom, bath, and kitchen until the rest can be finished, probably in spring. We'll see how the weather goes.

"Bessie has forgiven me. Actually went easy on me when she knew it was you and Helga. The thought of Helga next door and her new dream house has sure made her easy to live with. See? Everything has worked out fine, and won't Marguerite be happy when it's just her and Olaf in the big house? How can anything be better when all the women are happy?"

"Fritz, Helga and I have you to thank. How can I ever thank you enough? You were always, well, almost always my friend, even when I wuz drunk and broke."

I endured his bleary-eyed embrace and felt his damp cheek—or was it mine?—as I pushed away.

It was early the next morning when Helmer came by. I hadn't even shaved yet. I looked out to see him with a tape measure in his hand, checking the window framing.

I pulled on a jacket and went out. It was only November, but already the temperature was down and the frost had taken Bessie's flowers.

"Good morning, Helmer. You're out early."

"Yeah, Helga wanted me to come by and see how far along you are with your house. She's impatient."

"Yes, how well I know. Finally got it framed and it's begun to take shape, so Bessie is satisfied for the moment."

"Fritz, this house looks like it just growed right out of the ground, like it wuz alive. I never knew a house could go up so fast."

"It should go up fast—with eight men working on it. But it depends on the weather. Bessie keeps her nose in the plans—loves the big rooms, the windows—and she says the kitchen is a cook's heaven. But I'm going to claim the bathroom. No more trips to the two-holers through the snow for me."

"Well, Fritz, them plans must be catchy 'cause Helga is determined that we should have an indoor toilet too. Now Ila has jumped on the bandwagon, and I can't fight two wimmin. I aim to keep Helga happy. Come spring you'll hear some poundin' over here."

The weather held and the sound of hammers sounded from daylight to dark.

Two weeks before Christmas, we moved into our newly completed kitchen, bath and bedroom with the help of Olaf and Helmer. The rest of our stuff was stored until the house was completed.

A week later, Helga and Helmer moved into Helga's dream house. On Christmas day, everything was tidy. A big decorated tree stood proudly in our big kitchen window, competing with the one in Helga's dining room.

The women were ecstatic and living got easy. I smiled to myself. Ain't life grand?

A few days before Christmas, the pastor took sick with a bad cough and sore throat and could hardly make himself understood. Orren was home for the holidays so the pastor decided he should fill in for the Christmas service.

When the word went out that one of our own—"Orren, of all people!"—would replace the ailing pastor, the crowd gathered.

Fittingly enough, the title of his sermon was "Love thy neighbor." As I gazed over the congregation, I noticed more than one little towhead with the stamp of the Torgersons. Word was that Orren had flunked long division but got straight A's in multiplication.

Dressed in our finest, Bessie and I attended. Although we

came early, we found the church so full that we were relieved to see that Helmer and Helga had saved seats for us.

In the front row sat a pretty blond woman who was vainly attempting to quiet a little tow-headed boy and restrain his attempts to abandon her lap.

"Who's that woman?" I whispered to Bessie.

"She's Orren's wife, Chastity, and his boy. Shhh!"

"Watching, I saw him wriggle from her grasp and out of her reach with a few determined steps.

"How old is that kid, Bessie?"

I got a hard look from Helga and a very audible, "Shhh."

"Fritz, will you please be quiet? He's eight months old," whispered Bessie angrily.

"Eight months and he's walking?"

Helmer shot me a warning look and muttered, "Shut up, Fritz. He wuz premature."

I hid my hand under the hymnal and, as I counted back, I concluded that Orren had outmaneuvered the pastor at least once, but I heeded Helmer's warning.

"Orrie, Orrie," Chastity whispered loudly as she tried to look dignified as befitting a minister's wife when she pursued her son down the center aisle. I could hear old Gunther and Lars in the back row, "Ten to one on the boy…" I distinctly heard Olaf hiss, "Go for it, kid!" Then came Marguerite's "Shhh." I knew the Torgersons had a track star in the works.

Orren never hesitated as he strode up and down the platform and never stumbled on a word. But I saw him grin. He knew he had been upstaged by his son and he was preaching to the choir. He didn't give a damn. When the final prayer sounded, the congregation stood and clapped until the walls shook. I looked at the pastor, and I could see Orren's stock had hit the ceiling—if he only knew!

Christmas day dawned clear and cold. Thirty-two degrees. I looked out the window to see Helga waving the wooden spoon at the two boys who were struggling in the snow, a shiny red sled between them.

Apparently Frankie had spent the night, and the boys had surprised Santa at his task.

The snow glistened a pristine white and covered all traces of recent activities, even the stacks of lumber that waited until spring. It was as though the houses had always been.

The mouth-watering aroma that drifted from Bessie's state-of-the-art kitchen, the sounds of doors and drawers opening and closing, the clatter of pots and pans told me that Bessie was preparing her part of the Christmas dinner to be enjoyed at Helga's dream house.

"Do something, Fritz! Don't just stand there. Would you flip the lefse? Don't let it burn. Take the pies out of the oven if the crusts are browned, and put the cake in. Fritz! Don't slam the oven door—the cake will fall. Be careful, Fritz, look what you're doing for goodness sake. That was my mother's china bowl. Now look what you've done—get out of the kitchen…."

I could tell it wasn't going to be a merry Christmas for very long in that kitchen as I got the broom.

It was with a great sigh of relief that I joined the Torgerson clan in our old home.

Bessie and Helga disappeared into the kitchen. Orren, his wife, and son had arrived earlier, having spent Christmas eve with the old pastor who, I suspicioned, had some reservations about his less inhibited, newly acquired family, and so declined his invitation.

Then Olaf arrived with Marguerite and Baby Doll, who promptly retreated to the safety of Olaf's lap as Orrie pursued her, dodging among the tangle of legs.

Helmer, the genial host, seemed perfectly at ease. Black hair without a trace of gray, a clear, direct gaze, a tall man wearing a spotless white shirt, he was a handsome man who walked with natural grace and seemed to radiate happiness.

Orren regaled us with his exploits at the seminary, which almost made it seem like fun. Oddly enough, he seemed to really enjoy his radical change of lifestyle.

Olaf confided to me, "You know he's a natural. He's got that gift of gab, and since he knows how to change water into 'shine, he is probably of the opinion that will be his ticket through the Pearly Gates. Of course, he loves center stage."

Then we laughed as Orren said, "Look at my boy. He's got his father's good taste," as Orrie tugged at Baby Doll.

The aroma that permeated the room from the kitchen and the merriment that accompanied it made us salivating men suspect that the cooks may have been using more of the cooking wine than was necessary. Enough, hopefully, to erase all memories of Mrs. Melby's soup and her marital advice.

Orren said the blessing, Helmer carved the thirty-pound turkey that had roasted for countless hours. Helga and Bessie blushed at the extravagant, well-earned compliments for perhaps the best meal any of us had ever eaten.

Food, friendship, love, and peace. I knew this was the true meaning of Christmas.

We stayed the day, then left in the early evening. Helga and

Bessie, a formidable team, pushed us out. They had a busy day tomorrow. Olaf and Marguerite's day.

The wedding announcement made a month before from the pastor's pulpit gave the date and the invitation that all who wished to come would be welcome.

Olaf was the esteemed mainstay of the now thriving little town and how it buzzed with the happy news. It was Olaf, a favorite of both the French and Norwegians, who tamed the warring factions, which have merged to a most promising degree.

The congregation that crowded the sanctuary and overflowed into the entry grew quiet, except for the sound of someone stomping snow from his overshoes, the creak of the big door as it opened to a latecomer, the hushed whimper of a baby as it was quickly pacified.

I saw Lars at the organ, backlit by the soft light of candles. His hair was neatly combed—could that really be a white shirt? There was no spit can in sight.

I smiled to myself; Bessie surely had a way with her.

Looking about, I saw the old pastor sitting with his wife and daughter, trying bravely to restrain his adventuresome grandson. Earlier I had laughed when I heard him declare that Orrie resembled—unmistakably—his side of the family, but then admitted reluctantly that the boy was quite headstrong, "a trait he had inherited from his father."

My eyes drifted to Ila in her pink bridesmaid's gown, which fit her so well. I was surprised to see that she had obviously become a young lady. It seemed to have happened so quickly.

Orren, standing tall in the pulpit, blond hair shining, elegant in his robe, handsome as only a true Norsky can be, stepped to the pulpit, welcomed the waiting congregation, and gave the opening prayer. It seemed as though this was an accumulation of his life's ambition. I almost forgot I had known him when....

The organ sounded softly in the background.

I glanced at Helga. On her face was a look of such love and pride, which she made no effort to conceal. It took no revelation for anyone to know her years of sacrifice had created the foundation that made this moment possible.

I watched Olaf, with Helmer as his best man, walk down the long aisle to wait expectantly.

I escorted Marguerite to the groom, his smile wide, the scar unnoticeable.

Marguerite was breathtakingly lovely in her white dress, her veil secured in the black hair swept high, her big brown eyes brilliant with unshed tears and, in her arms, a bouquet of red roses.

Where had Olaf found red roses in this world of snow and ice in December? I could only guess. Perhaps St. Paul by Pony Express?

My duty finished, I seated myself with Bessie and Helga and immediately Baby Doll was deposited in my arms. It seems Bessie didn't want her new dress wrinkled.

The boys looked desperate trapped between the two women, but threatened by Helga's fierce look, they sat in mute silence. However, a quick pinch and a sly grin told me it wasn't a lasting commitment.

The quiet was broken by Orren's vibrant voice as he stepped from the pulpit to stand before his brother and his brother's choice.

His words were brief and beautiful in their simplicity.

Marguerite's tears found their release and flooded down her upturned face as she repeated the words that made her Olaf's wife.

"I take this woman to be my lawful wedded wife, now and forever, in sickness and health, so help me God."

Words spoken with conviction and sincerity that could not be mistaken. Words she had prayed to hear. These magic words: "I now pronounce you man and wife."

Lars fumbled, his calloused fingers searching the unfamiliar keys, then the soft strains of the organ rose to a crescendo as the memory was recalled from somewhere in that grizzled old head and the wedding march thundered with a vigor never known before.

The winter months stumbled by and the snow shimmered on the rooftops and lay heavy on the land. The sound of hammers had quieted, our house was finished, and Bessie was sewing curtains for our new windows.

I heard Buddy's anguished promises as Helga pursued him with the wooden spoon. It seemed he could not resist the sound of a flushing toilet.

Helga and Bessie enjoyed their morning coffee, trading recipes and confidences. With a knowing smile, Helga said, "Have you noticed Marguerite's apron seems to have shrunk?"

"No, but I have noticed that Olaf is going about grinning like an organ grinder's monkey."

CHAPTER 23

The next Sunday Bessie was trying to do something with her hair. I was still half asleep in my robe and slippers.

"Bessie, for heaven's sake, will you stop primping and put that coffee on? And can I expect breakfast today?"

We'd both slept in. We'd been doing a lot of that lately because, now that Helmer and Helga lived next door, we'd been visiting and staying up later playing cards. Last night had been late one.

"Oh, Fritz, is that the phone? Oh, it's Helga. She wants us to come over in a while, after the cake bakes and cools. She says Orren called looking for Olaf. She sent him out to the farm. Olaf will sure be surprised. We haven't seen Orren for quite a while. He is so busy with that big church, but says he will come by for cake and coffee. Isn't that nice, Fritz? Helga is so proud of him, and we'll get to see him too."

"Oh, yes, Bessie, of course I'll be glad to see Orren."

Orren, his love 'em and leave 'em pleasures of so many summers ago seemingly forgotten in the glamour and excitement of leading the largest and most prestigious church in Minnesota, is now a pastor who inspires the ladies in his congregation who hang on his every word.

The phone rang again as Bessie was fixing her hair. I answered this time and was shocked to hear Olaf's voice sounding a few decibels lower than that of a bull elephant.

"Olaf, Olaf! What's the trouble? Is everything okay with you? Calm down and tell me."

The phone went dead, but rang again immediately.

"Fritz, can I talk to you? I gotta talk to you. Can you believe this? I was down in the barn trying to show those damn chickens out—they're determined to crap in the hay. Then I heard Orren's voice and thought I must be dreaming. We haven't seen him in months and suddenly here he is in his big fancy car. 'Let's go out and look at your spring plowing,' he says, as if he ever gave a damn about the plowing.

"The tone of his voice was different, but I brushed away a momentary premonition. Hell, Fritz, he's been a minister for nine or ten years.

"I said, 'What a surprise.' Haven't seen or heard from you for quite a while—guess that big church must keep you busy. Ma is real proud and so am I. You're on the straight and narrow at last,' and I clapped him on the shoulder. 'How are Chastity and the kids?'

" 'She's gone,' he said, and then whined through the whole dirty story, Fritz.

" 'Well,' he mumbled, 'the path is still narrow, but it got a little twisty somehow.'

"Talk plain," I said. "What do you mean by 'twisty'?

"He stumbled around and talked fast.

" 'Well, well, I hate to tell you this, Olaf,' but of course he did, damn him!"

Bessie said it was then our lives started to unravel, thread by thread.

" 'There was,' he said, 'an awfully pretty seventeen-year-old girl who sang in the church choir. She tells me now that she is three months pregnant and her soldier boy has been gone for five months. Her mother—she plays the church organ—is blabbing to everyone in the church, and her father is the head deacon.'

"I blew it then, Fritz. I really blew it!

"I yelled, 'Damn you, Orren! Damn you to hell! You sanctimonious bullshitter with your big church and your fancy car. Don't you stand there with your hangdog look that I've seen so many times. Half the kids in the county look like you.'

"Fritz, I just grabbed him, but I wanted to hit him with my fist. Orren tells me to calm down 'for God's sake.' And I say, 'Don't you mention God's name to me!'

" 'Let go of me. Control yourself!' he says. 'It's really quite understandable when you give it some serious thought. Chastity is not the girl I married—she gained a lot of weight, she doesn't keep her hair nice, and she only has time for those hell-raising kids. And a man gets lonely. You know how it is. That girl was always under my feet, always in my way.'

"Fritz, I could have killed him on the spot. I've never looked—or wanted to look—at another woman since the first time I saw Marguerite.

" 'No, I sure as hell don't know how it is!' I yelled. 'Chastity has borne you five children—five kids in what? Ten years? Seems to me she's always pregnant, and Marguerite says she believes Chastity is pregnant again. Looks to me like you've had plenty of attention. Looks to me like you should have spent more time on your knees and less time on your belly.'

"Fritz, if I could get my hand around a bottle on short notice, Marguerite would have to hide me from the kids and put me to bed. I felt my hands start to shake and my fingers kept making fists.

" 'Now what the hell are you going to do?' I asked him.

" 'I don't know. That's why I've come to you. You were always good at fixing things when anyone picked on me.'

"When I could get the words out, I said, 'Orren, you know that hellfire and brimstone preacher will come after you with his shotgun. Chastity is his beloved daughter and all he's got besides the little church in town. He's pushing ninety-some years, but I'll bet he can still shoot straight.'

"I goaded him with that bit of comfort, Fritz, and I could almost see that devilish grin on Olaf's face.

" 'I know, I know,' Olaf said. 'How well I know. He's never really liked me.'

"And then his begging began. He said, 'Can't you take that gun away from him—impound it or something? Fix it for me, Olaf, for the good of the church. Think about Ma—you know how she loves me. Think about that, Olaf!'

"My voice, unrecognizable even to me, said, 'Hell, no! Never, never again. Got that? I'll never fix your fun again! You fix it yourself or face the consequences for once in your spoiled-rotten life. You fix it and leave the family out of it. Stay away from Ma and get off this property and stay gone or I'll shoot you myself!

"I saw him drive off in his fancy car. Well, Fritz, I can guess how this makes you feel, but you and Bessie are family too. Thanks, more than I can ever say, for listening. I'm going to drive over to Ma's and talk to Helmer too. But how in hell am I going to fix this mess?" his voice breaking into a sob I could have felt thirty miles away.

I felt drained of every emotion as I dropped the phone and let it dangle, twisting on its long cord.

"For goodness sake, hang up the phone, Fritz! Why are you just sitting there staring off into space? I've had time to curl my hair five times while you were on that phone—and you talk about us women!"

I was too disconcerted to answer. My stomach was about to revolt and I felt nauseous. I knew Helga would be heartbroken when she learned the bitter truth. She had hoped that Orren had grown past that love 'em and leave 'em way of life after all these years. I knew her problem would affect Bessie—they were like sisters. Then it would be my problem too, and heaven help poor Helmer. I knew the hard times we had suffered through wouldn't compare to this.

"Will you come on, Fritz? I've waited long enough."

"Bessie, I really don't feel well. Can't we go later?"

"Fritz, I want to see Orren and hear all about his big church. What's wrong with you? You're just put out because you had to wait while I did my hair. Well, you can just sit and pout. I'm going."

Resigned, I pulled myself up and held the door.

We walked over the well-worn path, and as we rounded the corner I saw a beautiful, shiny black Auburn Cord parked at the curb. My heart sank. I knew that Orren was here in open defiance of his brother.

I took Bessie's arm firmly, ignoring her surprised look. "Let's give Helga a little time with her son, shall we?"

She reluctantly agreed, and I nudged her to the porch swing. We sat, but Bessie, as always, was impatient. After a few minutes, she got up and wandered out to inspect Helga's newly planted garden, so I moved to a chair close to the window that I had rescreened so many times. I felt it slide open and Helga's voice sounded clearly.

"I'll just set this cake on the windowsill to let it cool, then we'll have cake and coffee. I'm so glad to see you I could cry."

I listened shamelessly.

I heard Orren's tearful voice. "Ma, I don't know how to tell you…"

Helga interrupted, "Don't tell me Chastity is pregnant again!"

"Only three months, Ma! It's not that, but she's gone to her daddy and taken the children."

"Well, the poor girl probably needs a rest. Five kids, Orren! I've heard that old preacher really loves those kids and plays with them by the hour, especially that little one who looks so much like Chastity. This might give her a little time to herself. What's on your mind, son?"

I peeked in the window to see Orren's head in his hands, then I heard his muffled voice blurt out the pitiful story that horrified Helga.

"Ma, there's this girl. She's seventeen and sings in the choir. She has been tempting me and pursuing me for months. The little she-devil is always rearranging my desk or straightening my robe and follows me around like a puppy. The more I try to discourage her, the more she clings. It isn't my fault, Ma!

Now she tells me she is three months pregnant and her soldier boy has gone off to war."

"When did he leave, Orren?" Helga's voice sounded hesitant, as though she were afraid of the answer but still held a faint hope.

"Five months ago, Ma."

I heard Helga's sharp intake of breath.

"Ma, that old preacher is going to kill me. Ma, will you make Olaf help me? I'm going to lose the church. That girl's mother is blabbing to everybody in church and her father is the head deacon."

Helga opened the door as if to breathe and saw me sitting there as Bessie walked back. Helga's strained face told me she knew I'd heard everything.

"You may as well come in. I'll make coffee."

We stepped in, and as we did I heard the sounds of Olaf's pickup. I pushed Bessie's indignant form to the sofa as I heard the slam of the pickup's door and, in an instant, saw the look of fury on his face. As Olaf burst through the door, Orren stood quickly to his feet, a shocked expression on his tearful face.

Olaf rushed across the kitchen and seized him by the front of his expensive shirt, shaking him like a rag doll and throwing him against the wall.

"How dare you bring your dirty laundry home to Ma! Haven't you learned yet to be man enough to be responsible for your own stupid actions? When will you learn? Will you ever learn?"

Orren struggled to free himself from the work-worn fist that held him captive against the wall, but to no avail.

"How do you dare to stand in that church and blaspheme God with your actions, you self-righteous hypocrite!"

The sound of the slaps that punctuated Olaf's words seemed to hang in the air.

Bessie and I sat as if glued watching a scene in a bad movie.

Helmer was desperately trying to restrain Helga as she struggled to get between her sons, her contorted face wet with tears.

"Olaf! Olaf! Stop! How can you treat your brother like this when he's come to us for help? Stop that right now! Shame on you! Apologize and shake hands. Let's see what we can do to help."

"Help? We've helped him all our lives. It's way past time for him to take responsibility for his own actions. I won't apologize. I can't, Ma, not even for you. He needs his ass kicked out of that church he has shown so little respect for, and I hope that girl's father beats the hell out of him if old hellfire and brimstone doesn't get to him first."

With that, he dropped Orren, who promptly found refuge with Helga and bravely asserted, "I'll have you arrested for assault, Sheriff!"

"Right," said Olaf. "I'll be in the cell next to the big-time preacher spending time for statutory rape. You know, if you could do it better the first time, you wouldn't have to do it so many times."

I snuck a look at Helmer and caught him sneaking a look at me.

Helga put her arms around Orren and said, "Don't worry, son, I'll visit that girl's mother. I'm sure we can figure things out and come to some agreement. Don't worry."

Orren walked out without a backwards glance, trying to close a shirt with buttons that weren't there anymore.

Helmer put his arms around Helga, saying, "Honey, let Orren sort this out himself like Olaf said."

She flung his arms away and ran sobbing to the bedroom. Bessie followed and I could hear the murmurings through the door.

Helmer poured me a cup of coffee, and I lifted it with a shaking hand, steadying it with the other.

"Seems like a long time—almost ten years, isn't it—since I poured you a cup of coffee, Fritz. No sugar lumps though." He grinned.

CHAPTER 24

That night the weather changed—everything seemed unsettled. Even the cows were uneasy, and the old cantankerous bull ceased his pawing and bellowing.

I looked to see the flash of the lightning that illuminated heaven, silhouetted against the ominous black clouds that hung heavy over Obeege. The air smelled of rain.

Our phone rang too early for a Sunday morning. It was just after five and daylight barely showed.

Bessie hurried to the phone. Alarmed, she said, "Get up, Fritz. We've got to hurry."

Later Helmer told me the beginning of the story that changed our lives.

"Early this morning the phone rang and rang. Finally Helga picked it up to hear Chastity's hysterical voice. She said, 'Orren has come home and told me everything. We are very upset, so I have come back to Daddy and brought the children. But he is taking us over to Orren's church today because I don't want Orrie and Marie to miss their Sunday School class.

They are almost old enough to be confirmed, so I must go. Could you come too and we can talk after the services?' Then she cried so Helga couldn't understand a word.

"I wasn't happy to be rousted out of bed at five o'clock on a Sunday morning, but when Helga told me to get up, I knew something was wrong—especially after yesterday's fracas. She said that we could make the eleven o'clock services if we hurried and to call you and Bessie and tell you to hurry too."

So hurry we did. Nonstop. Bessie and Helga sat in the back seat. Helmer and I talked politics and the possibilities of the spring crops. "Sure hope that south forty doesn't flood if we get a hard rain. My winter wheat is just starting to show."

We pretended we didn't hear Bessie's comforting words or Helga's broken-hearted prediction that Chastity would leave Orren and Orren would lose his church. "All these years he's worked; he's been so proud," Helga said, adding, "I haven't been able to reach that girl's mother," before her voice choked off.

I looked at Helmer, but he kept his eyes on the road. We both were remembering "love 'em and leave 'em." He nodded with just a trace of a grin when I whispered, "Pride goeth before a fall."

Helga continued the story as the miles rolled away. "Chastity called just as we were leaving this morning, and then called back. That's why we're a little late. If you want to hear Chastity's long, sad story, stay tuned."

"Of course," Bessie said encouragingly.

"Well, of course she came home to 'Daddy.' She's always been 'Daddy's Girl,' you know. And, of course, he was delighted to see her. Evidently he thought she shouldn't have driven so far by herself, though. He asked why Orren couldn't come and Chastity told him that Orren was very busy with his church. 'Too bad,' the old man said, and added that 'My old friend who is a deacon in his church tells me Orren is very, very busy—too busy, maybe. My friend keeps me posted about all the doings of that highfalutin 'church.'

"That old scoundrel is just jealous," Helga snorted. "Have you heard? Could you believe that when he preaches, he waves that bible in the air and stumbles around using his gun as a crutch? Some people think that's funny. I don't— it's sacrilegious."

I didn't dare look at Helmer, but he started to cough and I saw his shoulders shake a little. He said, "I can believe."

Helga went on as though she hadn't heard.

"With his usual tact, he asked Chastity if she was pregnant— and we hadn't even heard!" Helga sputtered. Then he said, 'When the good Lord said, "Go out and multiply, he didn't mean for you to do it all by yourself!" Well, she cried, of course, and, of course, he apologized. She said it was alright; she was just tired and the kids were fussing because they were hungry. She said she'd scramble up some eggs and asked if there was any milk; said she would just feed them and put them to bed, that they could talk then. You know, Bessie, I've never liked him. The old devil was so mean to Orren."

Helga paused for breath, and Bessie, unable to contain her curiosity, asked "What happened then?"

"Well, she got the kids fed and put to bed, while Daddy sat down and rocked the baby while she cleaned up. Then he told her to sit down and tell him why she's crying, that he knew she was upset.

"Chastity told me that she had dreaded to tell Daddy, but she knew it was going to come out soon anyway. She told him everything, she said.

"Soon enough," Helga said, "the way Chastity is carrying on, everyone will know."

Then Helga burst into tears again.

"Poor Orren. He already has to support five children and now she's pregnant again. Such a crybaby," Helga fumed. "Hope the kids didn't inherit that gene. It didn't come from our side. I had to listen to her boohoo through the whole thing.

"Chastity said, 'I had to tell him, Helga. I even told him that that girl and I are going to have our babies at the same time. Daddy's face just purpled and he rocked so hard the chair squeaked. He tried to talk, but the words wouldn't come. The only sounds in that silent room were my sobs and the chair squeaking so loud that it seemed to reverberate off the walls. I tried to tell Daddy that it wasn't Orren's fault.' "

Helga said, "Well, she's got some smarts."

"Chastity talked about the other girl to her father too. She told him, 'She is so pretty, she looks like I looked when I was seventeen. You can see that I've gained a lot of weight and I don't keep my hair nice—I'm so tired all the time. He really is a good man, but the women carry on so—always making such a fuss over him, and he just doesn't know what to do. Now this girl has seduced him! Daddy, I love him! I love him, Daddy!'

"But then her father stood up. Chastity said, 'I never ever saw such a look on his face. It scared me and he still hadn't said a word. Then he held the baby to me and said, "I'll put him to sleep." I answered, 'I'll take him upstairs...what did you say, Daddy? I didn't hear you right." He said, 'I've rocked him to sleep. Go to bed, Chastity.' So I carried the baby upstairs, laid him on the bed, and lay down beside him and slept.'"

Bessie looked hard at me, and I pretended I didn't see. The storm clouds had gathered, I figured.

Helga cranked down the window and exclaimed, "Oh, look Bessie! We're here, and it's only ten o'clock. Helmer, you must be tired from driving almost five hours. Let's stop and have breakfast; we have time."

It had been a nerve-shattering trip, at least for me, and I felt out of sorts. I wasn't hungry, but I knew if I didn't eat, Bessie would worry about my digestive system and take immediate plans to remedy it. We found a restaurant and had a good breakfast and, while Helmer and I had another cup of coffee, the girls found the ladies room and tidied up.

It wasn't difficult to find Orren's church. It nestled at the foot of a low hill, the elaborate spire pointed high. "Almost to heaven," said Bessie. The stained-glass windows were a blaze of color against the white of the church. The lawn was beautifully landscaped. Cars were parked in every available space. I had never seen so many people in one place.

The big bell summoned the faithful and we entered. Already, the church was almost full, but we went to the pews near the platform reserved for the pastor's family and listened to the organ music until the service started. The organ was played by a woman, the sight of whom caused Helga to nudge Bessie. They exchanged glances, and Bessie looked at the organist.

"Mrs. Olson, I believe," Helga said. "Orren told me she was good on the organ."

I looked around for Chastity and saw her come in carrying

the baby and with a small child clinging to her skirt. Her father followed her, leading a little girl who looked just like her mother. He seated them behind us, then turned and left. I felt a chill flush over me, like a winter wind.

The music played softly, the deacons filed in, announcements were made, certain events were highlighted, and then came the main attraction.

A collective sigh, soft as a summer breeze, was almost audible when the incredibly handsome young minister strode across the platform and opened his bible.

It was then that the clouds broke with all the fury of a tornado.

CHAPTER 25

The big ornate doors were flung open and old hellfire and brimstone stood for a moment like an avenging angel. He began his slow, deliberate steps as he advanced down the wide aisle, his shotgun held loosely, swinging at his side. A gasp swept over the congregation. Orren seemed transfixed, unable to move or speak. Somewhere a baby cried.

"You lying, cheating son of Satan. I want to hear the truth now." He continued his frightening walk, each step bringing him closer to the pulpit. Chastity started to rise, but his voice softly but sternly said, "Sit down, daughter, and tend your babies." Then his eyes returned to Orren and his slow, deadly voice boomed, his words paralyzing the elegant people.

"Pastor Torgerson, I'd like to hear a full accounting of your extracurricular activities these last three months. I think you owe it to your congregation; I'm sure they will be interested. Tell the truth and don't stumble. This old gun tends to go off if the truth is violated."

Orren stood as if turned to stone, his hand on the open

bible, his face white.

The lady at the organ stood up.

"Please sit down, Mrs. Olson. I'm sure you've heard this story already, but not from our godly pastor."

The head deacon rose to his feet, "Could we discuss this privately?"

"Not a chance! There was only one thing kept private and now it's going public."

The muffled sobs that dampened the ivory keys brought the head deacon to his wife, his arms around her hushing the sound.

As he continued his slow walk toward the pulpit, his shotgun was held a little higher.

"Pastor Torgerson, we want to hear your account, right now."

In a weak, frightened voice just above a whisper, Orren sputtered, "I, I, I want to…"

"Speak up, Pastor!" Daddy's' slow, frightening steps advanced.

"I want to apologize to my congregation for the shame I brought upon the church…three months ago…"

"More like four, wasn't it, Torgerson?"

"Yes," Orren agreed. "I was seduced by a woman…"

"Not yet a woman!" the old man interrupted. "A seventeen-year-old *girl*. Am I right, Mrs. Olson? It appears that your daughter and my daughter are both three months pregnant."

Abreast of the family pew, Daddy paused.

Orren stood silent, his eyes closed.

"Tell us what the bible says about carnal lust and adultery, Torgerson."

I held my breath.

Orren didn't look up; he stood wordless.

"Now! Right now, you son of Satan!" The click of the hammer as he lifted the gun sounded like a cannon in the quiet.

"Don't, Daddy, don't!" Chastity screamed as she squeezed out of her seat, her crying babies forgotten. Rushing up the short distance, she grabbed the barrel of the gun and held it to her breast, begging, "Daddy, please, please stop! Give me the gun, Daddy, please!"

Daddy fought Chastity's attempt to wrest the gun from his hands with tenacity. She held it with all the power of desperation. They struggled for the minutes that seemed like a lifetime to the horrified onlookers—the congregation was stupefied by the real-life drama. I could hardly breathe.

Daddy's grip loosened as Chastity yanked the gun from his suddenly limp hand. He staggered blindly, then fell headlong, sprawling on the carpet.

Later, the doctor said it was a heart attack.

Chastity looked confused, her long hair hung in her face, her clothing disheveled, breathing in great gulps. She looked at the gun in bewilderment, as though she had never seen it before. Then realization returned and she flung it away with all the strength she had in her body.

The gun flew through the air and struck a pillar, discharging with a deafening blast that shook the rafters and roused the faithful from their mesmerized daze. A beautiful stained-glass window shattered as though in protest of the sacrilege. The stink of gun powder, dust, and plaster permeated the air, and panic erupted.

Helga pulled away from Helmer and ran down the aisle to the platform, fell on her knees beside Orren's unconscious body, and held him to her, frantically trying to wipe the unceasing flow of blood from his head that soaked his vestment.

Helmer had stood helplessly, tears flowing. I knew they were for Helga's agony.

She looked up. "My God, my God, will this ever end?" Helmer knelt beside her.

Bessie had almost climbed over the pew to Chastity's frightened, crying babies.

I went to Chastity, who was holding Daddy. Her tears brought the tears, at last, to me.

She was begging him to wake up and giving his lifeless body little shakes.

Someone in the crowd that milled about like sheep had the good sense to call an ambulance.

I saw them load Orren in the ambulance and place Daddy beside him. They rode together in peace to the big hospital along with Helga and Helmer.

Bessie and I followed with Chastity, who was in a state of shock and whose tears never seemed to dry.

We all waited for the doctor for what seemed to be an eternity. When he finally came in, his tired face told the story before we heard the words.

"Mr. Torgerson is fortunate to be alive. Those lead pellets were terribly close to the brain, so time will tell. Obviously the gun must have been fired at close range."

I couldn't look at Chastity, whose hiccupping sobs were smothered in my handkerchief.

We took her home with us. Bessie held the three-year-old;

Chastity never relinquished the baby. Some kind lady in the church had taken the three older children home with her. When we left for our home, we picked up the kids.

The next morning as I sat with my first cup of coffee, I heard Bessie's surprised voice. "Chastity, your robe is stained…" An hour later, our local doctor had sent her to the hospital where it was discovered that she had miscarried.

Later, Bessie said that Chastity spoke plainly to the doctor and said, "Doctor, I don't want any more babies. I've got five. What can you do?"

"I can fix that," he answered.

Bessie was in instant agreement.

Four days later, Chastity sat at Orren's bedside and Helga came home.

"Bessie," Helga sobbed, "I can't bear it. This is more than I can stand. How long ago was I in the hospital with Olaf? And now Orren!"

Bessie tried to soothe her. "I know, Helga, it must be hell." Then Bessie cried.

Helga and Chastity took turns at the hospital sitting at Orren's bedside, waiting—for what? Chastity told Bessie, "I don't dare look at Helga. I think she hates me. Why can't she understand it was an accident?"

That made Bessie almost wordless. Bessie felt badly about that. Hasn't there been enough trouble in that family already? Only such a short while since Olaf and Orren nearly came to fisticuffs."

I couldn't answer.

Helga, who had survived Olaf's near death that hellish

night in the cornfield, now sat for hours in the hospital with her other son who lay with his face and head heavily bandaged.

After weeks of waiting, the grim announcement finally came. The doctor said, "The lead pellets that we removed from the left side of Mr. Torgerson's face have destroyed the nerves. Unfortunately, they will not rejuvenate. It was miraculous that we saved the vision in his left eye, but the eyelid will always sag, as will the flesh of his cheek. The ear was so damaged that it can never be restored. I can say he is fortunate to be alive. I am so sorry; we have done the best we could."

The doctor paused and wiped his glasses, then added, "He can go home in a couple of weeks."

Helga, who had alternately cried and prayed in Helmer's arms, stood stone-faced and dry-eyed.

Chastity fainted.

Ten days later, Orren disappeared.

Both Helga and Chastity had been notified and, of course, they were frantic. No one heard a word from him. Each day, each night, they waited. Chastity couldn't eat; Helga was never far from the phone.

Bessie was torn between the two. Chastity cried, "Helga hates me. She thinks I wanted to kill Orren! I could never, ever even think of that. He's the father of my children and I love him. I'll always love him. Why can't she forgive me? It was a horrible accident."

I thought to myself, *He was a damn lucky man to have two women like that in his corner.*

He had been gone over a month when a letter postmarked San Francisco arrived for Chastity.

It read: "Chastity, Have Olaf help you sell the Cord—you could probably use the money. I will send you more as soon as I can. Don't blame yourself—it was all my doing. You are better off without me. Find another life. Orren"

Helga received her letter the next day.

Olaf called me and said, "Marguerite has told me in no uncertain terms that you and Bessie are too old to take care of Orren's family—to have all that worry. She said she's cooking an extra chicken and wants me to come get them and bring them home. We've got lots of room on the farm, she added. Fritz! What in hell am I going to do with two wives and nine kids—her five and my four? Think about that!"

The next day our house seemed awfully quiet. Bessie slept almost until noon, and I had to make my own coffee!

I drove out to the farm the next morning. Orrie was carrying a milk bucket. The five-year-old boy was chasing the dog.

Marguerite called, "Fritz! Come in and have a cup of coffee. Olaf's around somewhere."

Inside I saw the oldest girl peeling potatoes, and Chastity was folding laundry. The three-year-old was helping. The baby sat in the same high chair that Olaf had bought for "Baby Doll"—how many years ago? And she's still his favorite, he confided to me later.

I went home with the happy news to Bessie, and she had happy news of her own.

Helga had called. She had driven out to the farm and surveyed the situation. Pointing to the five-year-old boy, she said, "I'd like to take this little man home with me. He looks just like his daddy. After all, we're family!"

She put her arms around Chastity, and they cried like they hadn't ever run out of tears.

When Helga was ready to leave and took the boy's hand, he looked at his mother. She nodded, and grandma promised him ice cream every day. When they drove away, he was smiling as he waved goodbye. Bessie asked Helga what Helmer thought about this and she said, "Helmer, the newly christened grandpa took to little Ole immediately, and the boy responded with so much enthusiasm that it brought tears to Helmer's eyes."

Later, Helmer told me, "This helps compensate for what I missed with Olaf."

That night Bessie and I celebrated—we played the phonograph and danced until at least nine thirty.

CHAPTER 26

A new day has dawned—it is 1941. The continuous rumblings of war in Europe since 1939, Hitler's deadly rise to power, the holocaust, the invasion and downfall of Poland—all that seemed so very far away to the inhabitants of the little backwoods town of Obeege. Churchill, fearing a German invasion, was pleading for Franklin Roosevelt's intervention. Although he helped in so many other ways, his land-lease program outstanding, Roosevelt was adamant in his refusal to go to war.

"I hate war," he had said in an address in 1936. "I have seen war. I have seen war on land and sea. I have seen blood running from the wounded. I have seen men coughing out their gassed lungs. I have seen the dead in the mud. I have seen cities destroyed. I have seen two hundred limping, exhausted men come out of line—the survivors of a regiment of one thousand that went forward forty-eight hours before. I have seen children starving. I have seen the agony of mothers and wives. I hate war."

We hunched over our little radios, reassured by Roosevelt's fireside chats and his reaffirmation that "I'll never send American boys to war."

It was the seventh of December. Bessie and I were sitting with Helga and Helmer in their front room. The girls were making plans for Christmas and trading recipes. We were eating chocolate cake and sipping coffee. Helmer and I were discussing politics—that topic never seemed to get old.

"Turn on the radio, Helmer. Let's see what Roosevelt is going to do about those ships that Churchill is begging for."

It wasn't long before we heard that Roosevelt has just announced that the Japanese had attacked Pearl Harbor.

Later, the horrifying details were released about the losses: nineteen ships, one hundred fifty aircraft, two thousand soldiers and sailors, one thousand two hundred civilians.

On December 8, the president declared war and thousands of young men enlisted the next day.

Twelve days later, Chastity received another letter postmarked San Francisco that read: "Chastity, if you need help for any reason, call Ma or Olaf. I know they will always help you. Forget me—you'll be better off. I was wrong, and I'm truly sorry to have hurt you. I have enlisted in the marines, and we sail for somewhere in the South Pacific tomorrow. Orren."

Blackouts, rationing, war bonds, defense plants—words on everybody's lips.

"Lucky for us," Bessie commented at breakfast one morning, "that Olaf and Marguerite keep the farm going. At least we have milk, cream, and butter. Thank heavens, no margarine—I hate to mix that stuff. Fresh eggs too, and always we have good garden stuff and fresh meat sometimes. Victory gardens are all over town, but rationing is hard on some."

"Yes," I agreed. "But I sure miss the gasoline and really good coffee, although I'm sure the fellows overseas need it more than we do."

Bessie was in a chatty mood as she bustled around the kitchen. "Ah, Fritz, did I tell you that Helga said she'd heard through the grapevine that the Olson girl had married her soldier boy? He came home from somewhere in the Pacific with one leg. Even though he isn't the father, he was crazy about the baby—a boy with yellow hair, Helga told me."

"Yes, I don't doubt it, and I'll bet Helga knows how much he weighed at birth too! Even the color of his eyes."

"Fritz! For goodness sake," was Bessie's indignant response.

The months passed; the war ground on.

"No! I don't want any more of that stuff that passes for coffee. What in hell do they make it from? I'm tired of this damn war—Roosevelt was right!"

"Fritz, did I tell you that Helga said Ila has gone to work at the Douglas Aircraft factory in Santa Monica. That's in California, three thousand miles away! Six days a week and ten hours a day for a dollar an hour. She wanted to join the WACs, but Helga put up such a fuss. She and Helmer just dote on Orren's boy—I doubt she will ever give him back to Orren when he comes home."

I didn't dare say, "What if he doesn't come home," but I knew if he was in the South Pacific, the fighting was bad there, especially on Guadalcanal where the casualty lists got longer. Gold Stars were displayed in so many windows. I read that the Office of Scientific Research has been experimenting with rockets and scores of new weapons, and the secret Manhattan Project has been busy working on a bomb that would change the war. *And that can't happen too soon,* I thought.

We read the papers, listened to the radio, and checked the casualty list. It seemed as if the war would never end.

Helmer and I poured over our maps. "I guess our boys must plan to fight their way up that chain of islands," Helmer said.

"Yes," I agreed," but the Japs seem to be so well fortified the closer we get, the casualties are so heavy."

I got a little shaky when I read that four hundred fourteen corpsmen had died on Saigon and eight times as many on Taiwan. I hid the paper from Bessie. Figured she might let it slip to Helga or Chastity, and I thought they had enough on their minds.

Buddy was driving Helga wild begging to enlist.

"No, no, no! You're not even sixteen—you're too young. I'm not going to let you go until you're eighteen."

"But, Ma!"

"Just because you're tall like the Torgersons...."

Helmer phoned Bessie one warm afternoon. "Can you come over right now?"

"What's the matter, Helmer. Where's Helga?"

"She's laying down in the garden—hurry!"

Bessie roused me from my map.

"Fritz, get up now! Come with me—something's wrong with Helga."

Helmer told me the story later. He said he had just come in from the field, and Helga was fixing some lunch when Buddy came bursting in.

"Ma, Ma! I've enlisted. I'm leaving Tuesday."

We were too surprised to say a word, then Helga screamed, "Buddy, you can't! You didn't! You're only sixteen—you're too young!"

"I know, Ma, but I did. I lied a little and told the enlisting officer I was eighteen. He did give me some trouble and told me to go home and come back when I'm eighteen. But I said, 'Honest, honest—I'm eighteen! I want to be a marine and shoot me a Jap. Send me to the South Pacific where they're fighting…'

" 'Are you sure you're eighteen?' he asked.

"Honest," I told him again.

" 'Well, you're big enough to be eighteen—you must be six feet if you're an inch.'

"Six feet one inch, and I weigh…."

" 'Never mind,' he said and he scribbled on some papers. 'Sign here.'

"I was so excited that I signed quick. I didn't even look when he handed them over. Then he said, 'Sailor you're in the navy now and you're a Seabee. We're building roads and airfields in the Aleutian Islands to keep the Russians out, and we need big, strong fellows like you.'

"I said, 'No, no, no! I want to be a marine! Where are the Aleutian Islands?'

" 'Alaska,' he said. Grinning, he said real loud, 'Dismissed, Sailor! Don't let the polar bears get you!'

"The guys in the line behind me laughed and pushed me out of the way. Ma, that line was a mile long. Frankie is gonna be so jealous!"

Bessie coaxed Helga inside. She took to her bed for three days until Helmer told her, "Honey, it could be worse. At least there won't be any Japs shooting at him."

A month later, Helga got a letter from Buddy telling her he was operating a big earth-moving machine and he liked it. Hadn't seen any polar bears, though.

Helmer laughed and said, "He was always good with machinery—remember how he fixed the tractor?"

Bessie told me that it was when Helga was washing her hair that the phone rang insistently, so she grabbed the phone with soapy fingers.

"Hello, hello, Ma? Ma, is this you? Can you hear me?

"Yes, yes, it's me!" said Helga, thinking her prayers were answered.

"Orren! Where are you? Are you all right? When are you coming home? Where have you been all these years?"

Helga told Bessie that she was so shocked that she could hardly speak.

"That will be the day," I snorted.

Orren told Helga, "We've had a stopover in Hawaii, but there's a planeload of us guys coming stateside on Saturday morning around ten o'clock. The plane should be easy to find. Do you want me to come home, Ma? Do you?"

"I will always want you to come home, son. Thank God, thank God," Helga said.

"Ma, I gotta go. This phone is in big demand. Only five

days, Ma—only five days."

He was crying when the phone went dead, Helga told Bessie.

Chastity said, "Why didn't he call me?" Helga told her that he probably thought she didn't want to talk to him.

"Of course I want to talk to him! I love him. I love him more than you do!" Chastity replied.

Helga said she let that go by, but she knew better.

Pandemonium erupted and plans were made. Helga's car got an oil change and two new tires. Helmer found gas coupons somewhere. I think neighbors donated. Marguerite planned to stay on the farm and take care of the kids. Bessie and I opted out.

They drove pretty hard, making the trip in four days, but Helga insisted she could have walked faster.

The big-time newspapers had received the information and got the word out: "A plane bringing a large group of wounded men from Iwo Jima expected to arrive at the San Francisco airport at noon on Tuesday. A large celebration is expected."

Preparations had been made—city dignitaries would give welcoming speeches, a marine band would play, a long yellow rope wrapped in yellow ribbon would swing in the wind to contain the anxiously waiting families.

The plane circled in, banked, the wheels touched down, and rolled to a stop. The uniformed band played "America the Beautiful," people in the crowd sang along, flags waved from everywhere. Excitement was at a fever pitch. The party from Obeege was at the front, the men trying to keep pace with Helga and Chastity. A ramp was quickly in place, the red carpet secured. The doors of the big plane opened and the crowd cheered wildly as men in wheelchairs—not boys anymore—started their slow descent.

It was the first time that America had a closeup and personal view of the boys who had gone to the battlefield perfectly and physically whole and returned so mutilated. These were the men who had left part of their body rotting on the bloody ground of a tiny island they had never seen before, nor would ever see again. They were dubbed "The Wheelchair Brigade."

The crowd quieted.

Then came the walking wounded.

Among the many uniformed men that crowded down, a tall, gaunt, white-haired man supported by a crutch, his chest decorated, his face in a twisted smile as his eyes searched the crowd. An officer walked with him, then halted and adjusted the microphone to speak.

"This man is one of the few corpsmen who survived Iwo Jima, where we lost almost seven thousand men. His commanding officer asked that I read this:

"Corpsman Orren Torgerson repeatedly disregarded his own safety and risked his own life to render medical aid to any section, to any zone of action. It would be impossible to estimate the many lives he saved. For this he has been awarded the highest medal in the nation—the Medal of Honor."

Chastity had seen him first and she was waiting at the end of the ramp, her arms flung wide.

Helga had tried to follow, but Helmer put his arms around her and said, "Honey, let her have this. She earned it."

People cried, flags waved, whistles blew. Photographers fought for space to set up their cameras. Reporters elbowed their way in, ignoring indignant looks.

On the way home, Helmer told me that he and Olaf felt abandoned in the front seat. Helga, Orren, and Chastity talked all the way home, and it was almost a four-day trip. The old car had only two flats, and the radiator steamed going over the mountains.

When things were slow down at Olaf's new office, I'd drop in and we'd talk for hours. Bessie waited dinner so many times she suggested I sleep there too. I said, "I would, but you'd miss me." She had to admit that was the truth.

Olaf had a reconditioned coffeepot from which he made coffee for us. And once in a while Helga would bring in a chocolate cake. When I told Bessie, the next day she brought one in too, fresh from the oven. Those two girls were still competing.

On one visit, Olaf laughed and said, "You know, Ma wanted Orren to do his recovering in town with her and Helmer, but Chastity, with a rare show of independence, spoke right up and said, 'No, Ma, he can recover with me in Olaf's bunkhouse and Orren agreed.' Then Helmer, with a half-embarrassed grin said, 'I think you should. The best time of my life was in that bunkhouse.' Ma was put out, but she had to laugh.

"Orren's recovery has been slow and steady, but he seemed so moody sometimes. I knew his leg hurt, and asked him once how it happened. He had never even told Chastity, but he answered me. He said, 'I worked among the wounded, screaming, bloody boys—too involved in their agony to fear or care if I lived or died. But that mortar shell made the decision for me. It tore the flesh from my thigh and my calf and finished with my foot—I nearly died. They sent me to a hospital in Hawaii.' "

On another day, after we had discussed the weather and complained about gas rationing, the price of war bonds, and the war in general, Olaf told me, "Frequently I would see a light in the barn, and I knew it was Orren. I would walk down and he would be sitting on an old milk stool staring off into space. He always seemed glad to see me, and I always had the feeling that he wanted me to hear what he wanted to say, but he couldn't find the words. When the words finally came, I found my own stool and sat with him.

" 'Olaf,' he said, 'I can't forget that hellhole. I still hear that never-ending mortar fire, the screams of the men on the bloody little island that the Japs regarded as sacred and that wasn't far from the homeland. You know, it took over a month before they put the flag up on a mountain, but I wasn't there to see it. That damn mortar shell with my name on it took me out. It was only because God wasn't done with me that I didn't die.'

"He stopped to light a cigarette. I could hear his loud breathing. With only the light of the lantern between us, his voice broke as he went on. 'Olaf, you were always the good one, always here for family and anyone who needed help. You've helped me more when you've been with me in this old barn, just listening, than all the good food. You've always told me only the truth and now I'm hearing it. You know, I lay there for months in that hospital, and I had a lot of time to think. I thought about the church that I had called my own for so many years, and the disgrace my stupidity had brought upon it. I knew they had disfellowshipped me—it was church policy. I thought about the shame I had brought to my family—my mother, who had sacrificed so long for us and was so proud of me. And what I did to Chastity shames me. I neglected my wife and my children.'

" 'As the hellish time passed, I swore to God, if he spared my life, I would make amends and be the man He wanted me to be.'

"Fritz, in my gut I believed him. He was honest for once in his spoiled, selfish life, and it took a war to do it. I turned the lantern down and went home to Marguerite and bed, and prayed he'd get the sleep so long denied him. The next day, he threw away the crutch. The good food, the outside time spent with his children, who always seemed to tag along with him everywhere, had given him a healthy tan and greatly improved his attitude."

It was as though a black cloud had lifted. Olaf was so unbelievably happy for him. For Helga, it was her prayers as it was Chastity's dream.

Bessie and Helga chatted nonstop.

My visits to Olaf's office continued and we argued politics. Sometimes Helmer joined us and it got really interesting. It was Helmer who brought the news that Franklin Roosevelt had died unexpectedly and that Harry Truman had become the United States president and commander in chief.

Olaf maintained that Truman didn't have the experience or the polish of the cultured Roosevelt, who had charmed the American public with his optimistic fireside chats, but agreed that "give 'em hell" Harry, with his plain talk and no-nonsense declarations, would leave no doubt regarding his intentions. Olaf added, "He's got the tenacity and disposition of a Missouri mule." Helmer raised his eyebrows at that.

Olaf's sentiments were realized not long after that conversation when Truman seemingly had no second thoughts or regrets about the results of the bomb that was so long in the making. The bomb, upon his orders, was dropped on Hiroshima and Nagasaki, Japan, and caused a level of devastation that had never been seen before in history and ended the war. The casualties, reported to be at least 129,000, was a hideous price to pay, I figured.

All America celebrated as did Europe when their country was freed from their inhumane leaders who themselves met with an inglorious death. Japan was an exception.

Two weeks later, the radio was dancing with the nightly news when Helga called.

"Bessie! Buddy is home—thank God, thank God!"

Helmer interrupted with, "And not a scratch on him. He's taller than Olaf, and I think he may be just as tough! Says he's ready to farm. He's sure a fine-looking man. He's growed up, Fritz."

Then Olaf added, "C'mon over—let's celebrate. I'll get a gallon of Bjournson's Best…"

"Count me out," Helmer said. "I ain't had a drink since Helga and I got married, and I ain't missed a thing."

We got so busy celebrating on hot chocolate that we didn't miss a thing either.

Helmer called me a short time after that and said, "Fritz, I guess you and I are in for another long drive. Hope this will have better results than the last one."

What is he babbling about? I wondered. Maybe he's

suffering from all that hot chocolate.

"Orren is determined to go back to that big church again. You know Helga and Chastity have tried to talk him out of it, but Helga's very unhappy and you know them, they always let him have his way. I guess they should—he's earned it, and he's sure straightened up."

He sounded a little apprehensive when he added, "There will sure be hell to pay if it doesn't go the way he wants it. Orren appealed to Olaf too. Orren begged, 'Can't you help me with Ma? She acts like I'm off to war again. I've got to do this, Olaf. I've got to try again. The church is my life. I'll be content to be the janitor—I can still manage a broom and dustpan if that's what it takes. Nobody will see this ugly face or even notice my limp. Surely you understand, Olaf, help me!' "

Olaf said, "Fritz, every man deserves a second chance." He went to town and bought a new tire.

But Chastity still persevered. She said, "I love him, Ma. I don't want him hurt, he's suffered enough, and they may refuse him. It's such a strict church."

She pleaded with Orren again and told him he had been disfellowshipped. "I got the notice when you had gone. You will have to go before the congregation and apologize. How will you feel if they don't accept it? Don't take that chance— you would be heartbroken. Would you ever forget? I beg you, Orren."

But he remained determined and made the arrangement with the minister who preached in "his" church.

Bessie was on Helga's side. She had reconsidered as Helmer had predicted, so I looked for my white shirt and a suit that would fit me.

Two weeks later, early on a beautiful Sunday morning, two carsful of us were on our way to "Orren's Church," as Helga still called it. The entire family—nine kids and nine adults, including Buddy who squeezed in—rode the long road to Bemidji.

We entered through the door where old hellfire and brimstone had made his surprise entrance that seemed so long ago. I noticed the church wasn't crowded. The ushers seated us near the platform that held the deacons and "Orren's pulpit," I heard Helga whisper to Bessie.

We filled the entire pew, and I heard the barely audible whispers and noticed the stares of some people that I assumed recognized us as the family of their previous minister.

Remembering the last time I had sat in this church, I couldn't get comfortable. Bessie stuck an elbow in my ribs and hissed, "Can't you sit still? You're worse than the kids!"

Looking around, I thought the church hadn't changed much—still big and beautiful. Obviously, a new pulpit and, of course, the new stained-glass window shined. I thought I could see where the plaster had been repaired on the pillars and I quickly looked away.

Glancing at Orren, I figured he had noticed that the church was only half full, and I knew beyond a doubt that he was thinking it was never anything but full when he preached. I saw the color mount in his face. I winked at him. He looked away, wondering, I am sure, how his thought was so visible.

The minister entered and walked to the pulpit; the congregation quieted when he opened his bible. Then the deacons filed in. I recognized Mr. Olson and, turning my head, saw his wife at the organ as she had been on that unforgettable day.

The minister gave the opening prayer, spoke of coming events, a hymn was sung. Then he made the announcement that brought Orren to his feet. I began to sweat.

"I'd like to introduce Mr. Orren Torgerson, who has come to this gathering with a request that I hope you will carefully consider. Please give him your full attention."

Orren struggled through the crowded pew, limped to the wide aisle, and faced the congregation. In a voice that had charmed so many now faltered. The words seemed to come so slowly, but the sincerity was unmistakable. The tears that he made no effort to hide glistened on his once-handsome face.

"I have come here this morning to apologize and ask you to forgive me for the disgrace that I brought upon this church. I am sincerely sorry, and I know that God has heard my prayers. My beloved family has blessed me with their love and forgiveness, and I pray that this church will do the same. I cannot walk alone.

"For the hurt and sorrow that I brought to Mr. and Mrs. Olson, I beg their forgiveness. I am so sorry, so ashamed."

His voice broke, his head bowed. He stood silently then, and waited. I didn't dare to look at Helga or Chastity, the two women whose lives were about to change regardless of the outcome.

I looked at Olaf and I knew he was with his brother, regardless of the decision that we all waited for.

The congregation sat silently as death, for an eternity it seemed. Then the murmuring began, but was stifled when Mrs. Olson stood, her face tear-streaked, and spoke clearly, "I make the motion that we accept Mr. Torgerson and invite him back into our membership."

A moment's quiet, then, "I second the motion."

The head deacon smiled at his wife and hurried down the aisle to put his arm around Orren and shake his hand.

"Welcome back, brother Torgerson."

I could see the tears that wet his face.

The congregation stood and broke into spontaneous applause and flooded around Orren with handshakes, hugs, and best wishes.

Bessie cried quietly through the entire event and held Helga's hand. Orren came for Chastity, his arms surrounding her. Her face glowed, and I thought how beautiful she looked.

Our trip home was a continuous celebration. Helga smiled all the way, her unwavering faith in her son at last vindicated.

Six months later, Orren was elected assistant pastor.

Our joyous family had arrived home and lingered with Helga and Helmer, who made coffee while Helga cut the cake. Bessie and I too tired to stay took our leave. We walked along the well-trod path now lined with soft-colored crocuses that pushed through the melting snow and promised spring.

I opened the door to "Bessie's" new house, and we made our preparations for bed. As I changed into my nightshirt, I watched Bessie roll her hair in those torturous curlers that she complained were hard to sleep in. I looked at her face and written on it I could see what our life together had been. Kahlil Gibran's words came to mind and I believed every one.

This is life.
Portrayed on the stage for ages;
recorded earthly for centuries;

lived in strangeness for years;
sung as a hymn for days;
exalted but for an hour,
but the hour is treasured for eternity as a jewel.
I kissed Bessie good-night and darkened the lamp.
Tomorrow is another day.

ABOUT THE AUTHOR

Dolores Durando, born in 1921, is the author of *And Yesterday is Gone, Beyond the Bougainvillea, Out of the Darkness,* and *Always in the Ribbons.* Her latest novel, *The Long Journey Home,* is loosely based on the author's own experiences growing up in North Dakota during the Great Depression.

Dolores gained deep intuition for the diversity of human nature as a licensed psychiatric technician in various mental hospitals for more than forty years. She served on mental health advisory boards, both in Califonia and Oregon, with fourteen years as a board member of *ASSET,* a nationally published magazine, for which she wrote short stories. She retired at seventy and moved to Oregon, where she has been writing, painting watercolors, and sculpting. She lives with her son and daughter-in-law in southern Oregon's stunning Applegate Valley.